ouise.'

e could feel her heart thudding. This close
him she was so conscious of everything
ut him—especially all those things she
n't want to be conscious of: his maleness
d her own vulnerability to it, the scent of
skin, the ache deep down in her own body
used by his proximity.

ne tried to push past him but he stopped
er, taking hold of her, and then she was in
his arms and he was kissing her—fiercely,
determinedly, almost as though he was laying
laim to her. And she was kissing him back.
Such a hunger possessed her, such a need,
such an aching, tearing, irresistible yearning
that she couldn't withstand its call. She wanted
to hold him, to touch him, to own him as she
had done all thos

impossible for her
nowhere to crush a

Everything she'd b
orgotten as the de ire only he could arouse
within her took control...

Penny Jordan is one of Harlequin Mills & Boon's most popular authors. Sadly Penny died from cancer on 31st December 2011, aged 65. She leaves an outstanding legacy, having sold over 100 million books around the world. She wrote a total of 187 novels for Harlequin Mills & Boon, including the phenomenally successful A PERFECT FAMILY, TO LOVE, HONOUR AND BETRAY, THE PERFECT SINNER and POWER PLAY, which hit the *Sunday Times* and *New York Times* bestseller lists. Loved for her distinctive voice, her success was in part because she continually broke boundaries and evolved her writing to keep up with readers' changing tastes. *Publishers Weekly* said about Jordan: 'Women everywhere will find pieces of themselves in Jordan's characters', and this perhaps explains her enduring appeal.

Although Penny was born in Preston, Lancashire, and spent her childhood there, she moved to Cheshire as a teenager and continued to live there for the rest of her life. Following the death of her husband she moved to the small traditional Cheshire market town on which she based her much-loved *Crighton* books.

Penny was a member and supporter of the Romantic Novelists' Association and the Romance Writers of America—two organisations dedicated to providing support for both published and yet-to-be published authors. Her significant contribution to women's fiction was recognised in 2011, when the Romantic Novelists' Association presented Penny with a Lifetime Achievement Award.

In May 2012 Penny launched the new continuity *The Santina Crown* with THE PRICE OF ROYAL DUTY. A SECRET DISGRACE is Penny's final original novel.

Recent titles by the same author:

THE PRICE OF ROYAL DUTY
THE POWER OF VASILII *(Russian Rivals)*
THE MOST COVETED PRIZE *(Russian Rivals)*

A SECRET DISGRACE

BY
PENNY JORDAN

MILLS
BOON®

First published in Great Britain 2012
by Mills & Boon, an imprint of Harlequin (UK) Limited,
Eton House, 18-24 Paradise Road, Richmond, Surrey TW9 1SR

© Penny Jordan 2012

ISBN: 978 0 263 89076 1

Harlequin (UK) policy is to use papers that are natural, renewable and recyclable products and made from wood grown in sustainable forests. The logging and manufacturing process conform to the legal environmental regulations of the country of origin.

Printed and bound in Spain
by Blackprint CPI, Barcelona

A SECRET
DISGRACE

CHAPTER ONE

'You say it was your grandparents' wish that their ashes be buried here, in the graveyard of the church of Santa Maria?'

The dispassionate male voice gave away as little as the shadowed face. Its bone structure was delineated with strokes of sunlight that might have come from Leonardo's masterly hand, revealing as they did the exact nature of the man's cultural inheritance. Those high cheekbones, that slashing line of taut jaw, the hint of olive-toned flesh, the proud aquiline shape of his nose—all of them spoke of the mixing of genes from the invaders who had seen Sicily and sought to possess it. His ancestors had never allowed anything to stand in the way of what they wanted. And now his attention was focused on *her*.

Instinctively she wanted to distance herself from him, to conceal herself from him, she recognized, and she couldn't stop herself from stepping back from him, her ankle threatening to give way as the back of her pretty wedged shoe came up against the unseen edge of the gravestone behind her.

'Take care.'

He moved so fast that she froze, like a rabbit pinned down by the swift, deathly descent of the falcon from which his family took its name. Long, lean tanned fin-

gers closed round her wrist as he jerked her forward, the
mint-scented warmth of his breath burning against her
face as he leaned nearer to deliver an admonishment.

It was impossible for her to move. Impossible, too, for
her to speak or even think. All she could do was *feel*—
suffer beneath the lava-hot flow of emotions that had
erupted inside her to spill into every sensitive nerve-
ending she possessed. This was indeed torture. Torture…
or torment? Her body convulsed on a violent surge of self-
contempt. Torture. There was no torment in this man's
hold on her, no temptation. Nothing but self-loathing
and…and indifference.

But her whispered, 'Let go of me,' sounded far more
like the broken cry of a helpless victim than the cool,
calm command of a modern and independent woman.

She smelled of English roses and lavender; she looked like
an archetypical Englishwoman. She had even sounded
like one until he had touched her, and she had shown
him the fierce Sicilian passion and intensity that was
her true heritage.

'Let go of me!' she had demanded.

Caesar's mouth hardened against the images her words
had set free from his memory. Images and memories
so sharply painful that he automatically recoiled from
them. So much pain, so much damage, so much guilt for
him to bear.

So why do what he had to do now? Wasn't that only
going to increase her deserved animosity towards him,
and increase his own guilt?

Because he had no choice. Because he had to think of
the greater good. Because he had to think, as he had always had to think, of his people and his duty to his family line and his name.

The harsh reality was that there could be no true freedom for either of them. And that was *his* fault. In every way, all of this was his fault.

His heart had started to pound with heavy hammerstrokes. He hadn't built in to his calculations the possibility that he would be so aware of her, so affected by the sensual allure of her. Like Sicily's famous volcano, she was all fire, covered at its peak by ice, and he was far more vulnerable to that than he had expected to be.

Why? It wasn't as though there weren't plenty of beautiful, sensual women all too ready to share his bed—who had, in fact, shared his bed before he had been forced to recognise that the so-called pleasure of those encounters tasted of nothing other than an emptiness that left him aching for something more satisfying and meaningful. Only by then he'd had nothing he could offer the kind of woman with whom he might have been able to build such a relationship.

He had, in effect, become a man who could not love on his own terms. A man whose duty was to follow in the footsteps of his forebears. A man on whom the future of his people depended.

It was that duty that had been instilled into him from childhood. Even as an orphaned six-year-old, crying for his parents, he had been told how important it was that he remember his position and his duty. The people had even sent a deputation to talk to him—to remind him of what it meant to stand in his late father's shoes. By outsiders the beliefs and customs of his people would be considered harsh, and even cruel. He was doing all he could to change things, but such changes could only be brought in slowly—especially when the most important headman of the people's council was so vehemently opposed to new ideas, so set in his ways. However, Caesar wasn't a boy of six any more, and he was determined that changes *would* be made.

Changes. His mind drifted for a moment. Could truly fundamental things be altered? Could old wrongs be put right? Could a way be found…?

He shook such dreams from him and turned back to the present.

'You haven't answered my question about your grandparents,' he reminded Louise.

As little as she liked his autocratic tone, Louise was relieved enough at the return of something approaching normality between them to answer curtly, 'Yes.'

All she wanted was for this interview, this inspection, to be over and done with. It went against everything she believed in so passionately that she was patently expected to virtually grovel to this aristocratic and arrogant Sicilian duke, with his air of dangerously dark sexuality and his too-good looks, simply because centuries ago his family had provided the land on which this small village church had been built. But that was the way of things here in this remote, almost feudal part of Sicily.

He was owner of the church and the village and heaven knew how many acres of Sicilian land. He was also the *patronne*, in the local Sicilian culture, the 'father' of the people who traditionally lived on it—even if those people were members of her grandparents' generation. Like his title and his land, it was a role he had inherited. She knew that, and had grown up knowing it, listening to her grandparents' stories of the hardship of the lives they had lived as children. They had been forced to work on the land owned by the family of this man who now stood in front of her in the shaded quiet of the ancient graveyard.

Louise gave a small shiver as she looked beyond the

cloudless blue sky to the mountains, where the volcano of Etna brooded sulphurously beneath the hot sun. She checked the sky again surreptitiously. She had never liked thunderstorms, and those mountains were notorious for conjuring them out of nothing. Wild and dangerous storms, capable of unleashing danger with savage cruelty. Like the man now watching her.

She wasn't what he had expected or anticipated, Caesar acknowledged. That wheat-blonde hair wasn't Sicilian, nor those sea-green eyes—even if she did carry herself with the pride of an Italian woman. She was around medium height, fine-boned and slender—almost too much so, he thought, catching sight of the narrowness of her wrist with its lightly tanned skin. The oval shape of her face with its high cheekbones was classically feminine. A beautiful woman. One who would turn male heads wherever she went. But her air of cool serenity was, he suspected, worked for rather than natural.

And what of his own feelings towards her now that she was here? Had he expected them? Caesar turned away from her so that she wouldn't be able to see his expression. Was he afraid of what it might reveal to her? She was a trained professional, after all—a woman whose qualifications proved that she was well able to dig down deep into a person's psyche and find all that they might have hidden away. And he was afraid of what she might find in him.

He was afraid that she might rip away the scar tissue he had encouraged to grow over his guilt and grief, his pride and sense of duty, over the dreadful, shameful demands he had allowed them to make on him. So was it more than just guilt he felt? Was there shame as well? He almost didn't need to ask himself that question when he had borne those twin burdens for over a decade. Had borne them and would continue to bear them. He had tried to make amends—a letter sent but never replied to, an apology proffered, a hope expressed, words written in what at the time had felt like the blood he had squeezed out of his own heart. A letter never even acknowledged. There would be no forgiveness or going back. And, after all, what else had he expected? What he had done did not deserve to be forgiven.

His guilt was a burden he would carry throughout his life, just as it had already been, but that guilt was his private punishment. It belonged solely to him. After all, there could be no going back to change things—nor, he suspected, anything he could offer that would make recompense for what had been done. So, no, being here with her had *not* increased his guilt—he already bore it in full measure—but it had sharpened its edge to a keenness that was almost a physical stab of pain every time he breathed.

They were speaking in English—his choice—and anyone looking at her would have assumed from the understated simplicity and practicality of her plain soft blue dress, her shoulders discreetly covered by simple white linen, that she was a certain type of educated middle class professional woman, on holiday in Sicily.

Her name was Louise Anderson, and her mother was the daughter of the Sicilian couple whose ashes she had come to bury in this quiet churchyard. Her father was Australian, also of Sicilian origin.

Caesar moved, the movement making him aware of the letter he had placed in the inside pocket of his suit jacket.

Louise could feel her tension tightening like a spring being wound with deliberate manipulation by the man watching her. There was a streak of cruelty to those they considered weaker than themselves in the Falconari family. It was there in their history, both written and oral. He had no reason to behave cruelly towards her grandparents, though. Nor to her.

It had shocked her when the priest to whom she had written about her grandparents' wishes had written back saying that she would need the permission of the Duke—a 'formality', he had called it—and that he had arranged the necessary appointment for her.

She would rather have met him in the bustling anonymity of her hotel than here in this quiet, ancient place so filled with the silent memories of those who lay here. But his word was law. That knowledge was enough to have her increasing the distance between them as she stepped further back from him, this time checking first to make sure there were no potential obstructions behind her, as though by doing so she could somehow lessen the powerful forcefield of his personality. And his sexuality…

A shudder racked her. She hadn't been prepared for that. That she would be immediately and so intensely aware of his sexuality. Far more so now, in fact, than…

As she braked down hard on her accelerating and dangerous thoughts, she was actually glad of the sound of his voice commanding her concentration.

'Your grandparents left Sicily for London shortly after they married, and made their home there, and yet they have chosen to have their ashes buried here?'

How typical it was of this kind of man—a powerful, domineering, arrogant overlord—that he should question her grandparents' wishes, as though they were still his serfs and he still their master. And how her own fiercely independent blood boiled with dislike for him at that knowledge. She was *glad* to be given that excuse for the antagonism she felt towards him. *No*—she didn't need an excuse for her feelings. They were hers as of right. Just as it was her grandparents' right to have their wish to have their ashes interred in the earth of their fore-bears fulfilled.

'They left because there was no work for them here. Not even working for a pittance on your family's land, as their parents and theirs before them had done. They want their ashes buried here because to them Sicily was still their home, their land.'

Caesar could hear the accusation and the antagonism in her voice.

'It seems…unusual that they should entrust the task of carrying out their wishes to you, their grandchild, in-stead of your mother, their daughter.'

Once again he was aware of the pressure of the letter in his pocket. And the pressure of his own guilt…? He had offered her an apology. That was the past and it must remain the past. There was no going back. The guilt he felt was a self-indulgence he could not afford to recog-nise. Not when there was so much else at stake.

'My mother lives in Palm Springs with her second husband, and has done so for many years, whilst I have always lived in London.'

'With your grandparents?'

Even though it was a question, he made it seem more like a statement of fact.

Was he hoping to provoke her into a show of hostility he could use against her to deny her request? She cer-tainly didn't trust him not to do so. If that was indeed his aim, she wasn't going to give him the satisfaction. She could hide her feelings well. She had, after all, a wealth of past experience to fall back on. That was what happened when you were branded as the person who had brought so much shame on her family that her own parents had turned their back on you. The stigma of that shame would be with her for ever, and it deprived her of the right to claim either pride or privacy.

'Yes,' she confirmed, 'I went to live with them after my parents divorced.'

'But not immediately after?'

The question jolted through her like an arc of electricity, touching sensitive nerve-endings that should have been healed. Not that she was going to let *him* see that.

'No,' she agreed. But she couldn't look at him as she answered. Instead she had to look across the graveyard— so symbolic, in its way, as a graveyard of her own longings and hopes which the end of her parents' marriage had brought about.

'At first you lived with your father. Wasn't that rather unusual for a girl of eighteen? To choose to live with her father rather than her mother?'

Louise didn't question how he knew so much about her. The village priest had requested a history of her family from her when she had written to him with regard to the burial of her grandparents' ashes. Knowing the habits of this very close Sicilian community, she suspected enquiries would have also been made via contacts in London.

The thought of that was enough to have fully armed anxiety springing to life inside her stomach. If she couldn't fulfil her grandparents' final wishes because this man chose to withhold his permission because of *her*...

Automatically Louise bowed her head, her golden hair catching the stray beams of sunlight penetrating the green darkness of the cypress-shaded graveyard.

It had been an unwelcome shock, and the last thing she had felt prepared for, to see *him*, and not the priest as she had anticipated. With every look he gave her, every silence that came before another question, she was tensing her nerves against the blow she knew he could deliver. Her desire to turn and flee was so strong that she was trembling inside as she fought to resist it. Fleeing would be as pointless as trying to outrun the deathly outpouring from a volcano. All it would achieve would be a handful of heart-pounding, stomach-churning, sickening minutes of time in which to imagine the awfulness of her fate. Better, surely, to stand and defy it and at least have her self-respect intact.

All the same, she had to grit her perfectly straight, neat white teeth very hard to stop herself giving vent to her real feelings. It was none of his business that she and her mother had never been close, with her mother always being far more concerned with her next affair or party than having a conversation with her daughter. In fact she'd been absent more than present throughout Louise's life. When her mother had announced she was leaving for Palm Springs and a new life Louise had honestly felt very little other than a faint relief. Her father, of course, was rather a different story—his constant presence served as an endless reminder of her own failings.

It was a moment before she could bring herself to say distantly, 'I was in my final year of school in London when my parents divorced, so it made sense for me to move in with my father. He had taken a service apartment in London, since the family house was being sold and my mother was planning to move to Palm Springs.'

His questions were far too intrusive for her liking, but she knew that to antagonise this man—even if she *was* coming to resent him more with every nerve-shattering dagger-slice he made into the protective shield she had wrapped around her past—would prove to be counterproductive. She was determined not to do so.

All that mattered about this interview was getting this arrogant, hateful overlord's agreement to the burial of her grandparents' ashes in accordance with their wishes. Once that was done she could give vent to her own feelings. Only then could she finally put the past behind her and live her own life, in the knowledge that she had discharged the almost sacred trust that had been left to her.

Louise swallowed hard against the bitter taste in her mouth. How she had changed from that turbulent eighteen-year-old who had been so governed by emotion and who had paid such a savage price.

She still hated even *thinking* about those stormy years, when she'd witnessed the breakdown of her parents' marriage and the resulting fall-out, never mind being forced to talk about it. That fall-out had seen her passed like an unwanted parcel between her parents' two separate households, welcome in neither and especially unwelcome where her father's new girlfriend had been concerned. As a result of which, according to both her parents and their new partners, she had brought such shame on them that she had been no longer welcome in the new lives they were building for themselves.

Looking back, it was no wonder that her parents had considered her to be such a difficult child. Was it because her father's work had made him an absent father that she had tried so desperately to win his love? Or had she known instinctively at some deep atavistic level even then that her conception and with it his marriage to her mother had always been bitterly regretted and resented by him?

A brilliant young academic, with a glowing future ahead of him, the last thing he had wanted was to be forced into marriage with a girl he had got pregnant. But pressure had been brought to bear on him by a Senior Fellow at Cambridge whose family had also been members of London's Sicilian community. The brilliant young Junior Research Fellow had been obliged to marry the pretty student who had seen him as an escape from the strictures of an old-fashioned society or risk having his career blighted.

Louise didn't consider herself to be Sicilian, but perhaps there was enough of that blood in her veins for her always to have felt not just the loss of love but also the public humiliation that came from not being loved by her father. Italian men—Sicilian men—were usually protective and proud of the children they fathered. Her father had not wanted her. She had got in the way of his plans for his life. As a crying, clingy child and then a rebellious, demanding teenager she had first irritated and then annoyed him. For her father—a man who had wanted to travel and make the most of his personal freedom— marriage and the birth of a child had always been shackles he did not want. Because of that alone her attempts to command her father's attention and his love had always been doomed to failure.

Yet she had clung determinedly to the fictional world she had created for herself—a world in which she was her father's adored daughter. She'd boasted about their relationship at the exclusive girls' school her mother had insisted on sending her to, with daughters of the titled, the rich and the famous, clinging fiercely to the kudos that went with having such a high-profile and good-looking parent. He'd had a role as the front man of a hugely popular quasi-academic TV series, which had meant that her fellow pupils accepted her only because of him.

Such a shallow and fiercely competitive environment had brought out the worst in her, Louise acknowledged. Having learned as a child that 'bad' behaviour was more likely to gain her attention than 'good', she had continued with that at school, deliberately cultivating her 'bad girl' image.

But at least her father had been there in her life, to be claimed as being her father—until Melinda Lorrimar, his Australian PA, had taken him from her. Melinda had been twenty-seven to Louise's eighteen when they had gone public with their relationship, and it had perhaps been natural that they should compete for her father's attention right from the start.

How jealous she had been of Melinda, a glamorous Australian divorcee, who had soon made it clear that she didn't want her around, and whose two much younger daughters had very quickly taken over the room in her father's apartment that was supposed to have been hers. She had been so desperate to win her father's love that she had even gone to the extent of dying her hair black, because Melinda and her girls had black hair. Black hair, too much make-up and short, skimpily cut clothes—all an attempt to find a way to be the daughter she had believed her father wanted, an attempt to find the magic recipe that would turn her into a daughter he could love.

Her father had obviously admired and loved his glamorous PA, so Louise had reasoned that if she were more glamorous, and if men paid her attention, then her father would be bound to be as proud of her as he was of Melinda and as he had surely once been of her mother. When that had failed she'd settled for trying to shock him. Anything was better than indifference.

At eighteen she had been so desperate for her father's attention that she'd have done anything to get it— anything to stop that empty, hungry feeling inside her that had made it so important that she succeed in becoming her father's most loved and cherished daughter instead of the unloved failure she had felt she was. Sexually she had been naive, all her emotional intensity invested in securing her father's love. She'd believed, of course, that one day she would meet someone and fall in love, but when she did so it would be as her father's much loved daughter, someone who could hold her head up high—not a nuisance who was constantly made to feel that she wasn't wanted.

That had been the fantasy she'd carried around inside her head, never realising how dangerous and damaging it was, because neither of her parents had cared enough about her to tell her. To them she had simply been a re-minder of a mistake they had once made that had forced them into a marriage neither of them had really wanted.

'But when you started your degree you were living with your grandparents, not your father.'

The sound of Caesar Falconari's voice brought her back to the present.

An unexpected and dangerous thrill of sensation burned through her—an awareness of him as a man. A man who wore his sexuality as easily and unmistakably as he wore his expensive clothes. No woman in his pres-ence could fail to be aware of him as a man, could fail to wonder...

Disbelief exploded inside her, caused by the shock of her treacherous awareness of him. Where on earth had it come from? It was so unlike her. So... Sweat beaded her forehead and her body was turning hot and sensually tender beneath her clothes. What was happening to her? Panic rubbed her nerve-endings as raw as though they had been touched with acid. This wasn't right. It wasn't... wasn't *permissible*. It wasn't...wasn't *fair*.

A stillness like the ominous stillness that came just before the breaking of a storm gripped her. This should not be happening. She didn't know why it was. The only awareness of him she could permit herself to have was an awareness of how dangerous and damaging he could be to her. She must *not* let him realise the effect he was having on her. He would enjoy humiliating her. She knew that.

But she wasn't an emotionally immature eighteen-year-old any more, she reminded herself as she struggled to free herself from the web of her own far too vulnerable senses to find safer ground.

'As I'm sure you know, given that you obviously know so much about my family history, my bad behaviour—especially with regard to my father's new wife-to-be and the impact she felt it might have on her own daughters—caused my father to ask me to leave.'

'He threw you out.'

Caesar's response was a statement, not a question.

There it was again—that twisting, agonising turning of the knife in a new guilt to add to the old one he already carried.

Given that for the last decade he had dedicated himself to improving the lot of his people, what he had learned about Louise and the uncaring and downright cruel behaviour she had been subjected to by those who should have loved and protected her, could never have done anything other than add to his burden of guilt. It had never been his intention to hurt or damage her—far from it—and now, knowing what he did, he could well understand why she had never responded to that letter he had sent, acknowledging his guilt and imploring her to forgive him.

It went against the grain of everything that being a Sicilian father meant to abandon one's child, yet at the same time for a family to be so publically shamed by the behaviour of one of its members left a stain on that family's name that would be passed down unforgotten and unforgiven throughout the generations.

Louise could feel her face starting to burn. Was it through guilt or a still-rebellious sense of injustice? Did it matter? It certainly shouldn't. The counselling she had undergone as part of the training for her career as a much sought after reconciliation expert, working to help bring fractured families back together again, had taught her the importance of allowing oneself errors of judgement, acknowledging them, and then moving on from them.

'He and Melinda had plans to start a new life together in Australia. It made sense for him to sell the London apartment. Technically I was an adult anyway, as I was eighteen. I was going to university. But, yes, in effect he threw me out.'

So she had been left alone and uncared for whilst *he* had been on the other side of the world, learning all he could about improving the lot of the poorest people in that world in a bid to expiate his guilt and find a new way of living his life that would benefit his own people.

There was no point in telling her any of that, though. It was plain how antagonistic she was towards him and anything he might have to say.

'And that was when you moved in with your grandparents?' he continued. It was, after all, easier to stick to practicalities and known facts than to stray onto the dangerous unstable territory of emotions.

Louise felt the tension gripping her increase. Hadn't he already done enough, damage, hurt and humiliated her enough without dragging up the awfulness of the past?

Even now she could hardly bear to think about how frightened she had been, or how abandoned and alone she had felt. Her grandparents had saved her, though. With the love they had shown her, they had rescued her.

That had been the first time in her life she had truly understood the importance of giving a child love and security, and all that family love could mean. That was when her whole life had changed and she herself with it. That was when she had promised herself that, whatever it took, one day she would repay her grandparents for their love for her.

'Yes.'

'That must have been a very brave gesture on their part, given…'

'Given what I had done? Yes, it was. There were plenty of people in their local community who were ready to criticise and condemn them, just as they had already condemned me. I had brought shame on my grandparents and by association could potentially bring shame on their community. But then you know all about that, don't you? You know how shamefully and shockingly I behaved, and how I humiliated and damaged not just myself but my grandparents and all those connected with them. You know how my name became a byword for shame in our community and how my grandparents suffered for that. Suffered for it but still stood by me. And because of that you will also know why I am here now, enduring this further humiliation by you.'

He wanted to say something—to tell her how sorry he was, to remind her that he had tried to apologise— but at the same time he knew that he had to stand strong. There was far more at stake here than their own emotions. Whether they liked it or not they were both part of a much greater pattern, their lives woven into the fabric of the society into which they had both been born. That was something neither of them could ignore or walk away from.

'You want to carry out the promise you made to your grandparents that their ashes will be buried here?'

'It was what they always wanted, and of course it became more important to them after…after the shame I brought them. Because burial of their ashes here was their only means of returning to being fully accepted members of their community, being accepted as having the right to be at rest here in the church in which they were christened, confirmed and married. There is nothing I will not do to make that happen—even if that means having to beg.'

Caesar hadn't expected her honesty. Hostility and antagonism towards him, yes, he had expected those, but her honesty had somehow slipped under his guard. Or was it that part of him—the modern, educated part, that was constantly striving to align the desire to bring his people into the twenty-first century with being custodian of their ancient customs—was looking on with modern-day compassion? This was a young girl caught up in a system of values that had punished her for modern-day behaviour that contravened the old rules.

He could feel the weight of the letter in his pocket. Like pressure on a raw wound, grinding into it painfully sharp shards of broken glass.

She was beginning to lose her self-control, Louise recognised. That mustn't happen. She must accept that, whilst it was only natural that she shouldn't want to answer him, she must resist the impulse to be defensive. What mattered was the debt of love she owed her grandparents, and no one—especially not this arrogant, lordly Sicilian, whose very presence in the same airspace as her was causing her body to react with angry contempt—was going to compromise that. After all, given what she had already been through, what was a little more humiliation? The words *straw*, *broke* and *camel's back* slid dangerously into her mind, lodging there like small yet effective barbs.

She had almost been out of her mind with shock and shame and anger when her grandparents had taken her in, incapable of *thinking* for herself, never mind looking after herself. She had virtually crawled into bed, barely noticing the bedroom they had given her in their pretty Notting Hill house—the house they had bought so proudly when, after years of working for others, their restaurant had finally made them financially independent. She had wanted only to hide away from everyone. Including herself.

Her grandparents and their house had been her sanctuary. They had given her what she had been denied by both her mother and her father. They had taken her in and loved her when others had rejected her, ashamed *of* her and *for* her. *Shame.* Such a terrible word to a proud Sicilian. The scar that covered her shame throbbed angrily and painfully. She'd have done anything rather than come here, but she owed her grandparents so much.

In all the calculations she had made about what might be asked of her, what penance she might have to pay in order to remove the stain of dishonour from their family name and win agreement for the burial of her grandparents' ashes, she had never thought to factor in the fact that she would be confronted by this man and forced to answer to him for her sins. The truth was that she had thought he'd be as antagonistic towards such a meeting as she was herself. She had obviously underestimated his arrogance.

'As you know, I alone am not responsible for any decision made with regard to your request. The village elders—'

'Will take their cue from you. As you must know perfectly well that I know that. You are the one who holds the authority to grant my grandparents' request. To deny them this, their chosen final resting place, would be beyond unfair and cruel. To punish them because—'

'That is the way of our society. The whole family suffers when one member of it falls from grace. You know that.'

'And you think that is *right*?' she demanded scornfully, unable to prevent herself from saying acidly, 'Of course you do.'

'Here in this part of Sicily people live their lives to rules and customs that were laid down centuries ago. Of course I can see many faults in those customs and rules, and of course I want to assist in changes that will be for the benefit of my people, but those changes can only come about slowly if they are not to lead to distrust and unhappiness between the generations.'

Louise knew that what he was saying was true, even if she didn't want to admit it. Even if something in the trained, professional part of her was thinking eagerly of the opportunities for good that must surely come from being in a position to put in place changes that would ultimately benefit so many people and help them to understand and reach out for the gifts of the future, whilst laying to rest the ghosts of the past. Besides it was her grandparents' wishes she wanted to discuss with him.

'My grandparents did a great deal for their community. In the early days they sent money home here, for their parents and their siblings. They went without to do that. They employed people from the village who came to London. They housed them and looked after them. They gave generously to the church and to charity. It is their right to have all that they were and all that they did recognised and respected.'

She was a passionate advocate for her grandparents, and he couldn't doubt the strength of her feelings, Caesar acknowledged. A discreet bleep from his mobile phone warned him of an impending appointment. He hadn't expected this interview with her to take as long as it had, and there were still things he needed to say—questions he needed to ask.

'I have to go. I have an appointment. However, there are things we still need to discuss,' he told her. 'I shall be in touch with you.'

He was turning to walk away, having made it clear that he intended to keep her on edge and anxious. A cruel act from a man who had cruelty and pride bred into his blood and his bones. Perhaps she shouldn't have expected anything else. And the relief she felt because he was going? What did *that* say about her and her own reserves of strength?

He was only a couple of metres away from her when he turned. The sun slanting through the cypresses caught against the sharp, hard bones of his face, throwing it into relief so that he looked as if he could easily have traded places with one of his own fierce warrior ancestors—that toxic mix of pre-Christian Roman and Moor was stamped clearly on his features.

'Your son,' he said. 'Have you brought him to Sicily with you?'

CHAPTER TWO

WAS this how it felt when the sky fell in on you? And yet she should have been prepared for such a question.

'Yes.' Her answer was terse, because that one word was all she could manage with the angry fear that was crawling with sickening intensity through her veins. Not that she had anything to fear. It was no secret, after all, that she was a single mother with a nine-year-old son.

'But you didn't choose to bring him here with you? Was that wise? He is only nine years old. A responsible mother—'

'As a "responsible mother" I decided that my son would be safer and happier, whilst we conducted our interview, keeping his appointment for a tennis lesson as part of the children's club activities provided by our hotel. Oliver, my son, was very close to his great-grandfather. He misses him. Bringing him here today wouldn't have helped Ollie.'

Even if he could have been persuaded to come.

She was shaking inside with mortified anger, but she wasn't going to let him see it. She couldn't let him see it. The truth was that for the last eighteen months her relationship with Ollie had been going through an increasingly difficult time, with Oliver making it *very* plain to her that he blamed her for the fact that he didn't have a father. This had led to problems at school, with Ollie getting into trouble because of arguments and scraps with other boys who *did* have fathers in their lives, and a painful gulf was growing between her and the son she loved so very much.

She would have done anything to protect Ollie from the pain he was going through—*anything*. She loved her work, and was proud of what she had achieved—of course she was—but she knew that without Ollie to be responsible for she would probably never have pushed herself to go back into education, get her qualifications and then start to climb the career ladder. It was for Ollie that she had worked long into the night, studying and working, so that she would always be able to provide him with a secure financial future. But what Ollie was now insisting he wanted more than anything else was the one thing she could not give him. A father.

Whilst her grandfather had been alive he had been able to provide a stabilising and loving male influence in Ollie's life, but even then Ollie had started to become withdrawn and angry with her because she would not give him any information about his father.

Oliver was a clever boy at a good school. The private fees soaked up a large part of her income. But even though there were plenty of other boys there whose fathers were absent from their lives for one reason or another, unlike Oliver they at least seemed to have some contact with those fathers. Her grandfather had been very concerned about the effect the lack of any information about his father was having on Oliver, but he had known as well as she did how impossible it was for her to tell Ollie the truth—and she certainly wasn't prepared to lie to him by concocting a comforting, sanitised version.

Louise loved her son. There wasn't anything she wouldn't

do for him to make him happy. But she couldn't tell him about his father. At least not yet—not until he was old enough to understand something of the demons that had driven her. And old enough to forgive her for them. Her transgressions might not have given him a father, but they— and the loving care of his great-grandparents, who had stood by her when she had totally refused to have the termination her parents had tried to insist on—had given him life. Surely that was a gift worth having?

'We still have things to discuss. I shall call on you at your hotel tomorrow morning at eleven o'clock in the coffee shop.'

Not a single word as to whether or not it might be convenient for her to see him at eleven o'clock, or indeed if she would have preferred to meet him somewhere else. But what else had she expected? Arrogance was this man's middle name—along with cruelty and overweening pride. It was a great pity that someone didn't cut the all-powerful, judgemental Duca di Falconari down to size and make him as mortal and vulnerable as those he obviously thought so far beneath him.

From the churchyard Louise could just see the polished shine of the black metal bonnet of the waiting limousine as it drew away, the dark-tinted windows obscuring any view she might have had of its passenger. Not that she wanted to look at him, or indeed have anything to do with him, but she had no choice.

From the path that wound through the hotel's gardens and ran past the tennis courts Caesar had a good view of the young boy who had just arrived as part of a group under the care of the hotel's children's club team, to begin a lesson with one of the hotel's tennis coaches.

Louise Anderson's son. He was tall and strongly muscled for his age, and he hadn't inherited his mother's colouring Caesar recognised. The boy was olive-skinned and dark-haired—but then that was hardly surprising given his Sicilian blood. He was a good player, focused and with a strong backhand.

Caesar looked at his watch and quickened his pace. He had taken a roundabout route to the hotel coffee shop, knowing it would take him past the tennis courts, and he didn't want to be late for his appointment with Louise. As always when he thought about her he could feel his long-standing burden of guilt and regret.

Louise checked her watch. Eleven o'clock. Her son had been surprised and pleased when she had suggested that he have another tennis lesson. Such lessons were 'extras' on top of their holiday budget, and she'd warned him before they came that there wouldn't be much money for such things. A stab of guilt stung her conscience. Right now she needed to be spending time with Ollie and trying to find a way to put things right between them. Wasn't that exactly the kind of advice she would be giving another parent in her circumstances? The trouble was that child-rearing was easier when it was shared not just between two parents but with an extended family. And she and Ollie only had one another.

Louise closed her eyes briefly as she sat on one of the banquettes in the hotel coffee shop. She missed both her grandparents dreadfully, but especially her grandfather. And if *she* missed his wise, loving kindness and guidance then how much more must Ollie miss him?

They had been close, the two of them, and now Ollie had no male influence on his life to guide and love him.

When she opened her eyes again she saw that Caesar Falconari was striding towards her. More casually dressed today, he was still looking very Italian in his buff-coloured linen jacket, black tee shirt and light-coloured chinos. No other man but an Italian could carry off such an outfit with so much cool sexuality. It was no wonder that every female head within looking distance swivelled in his direction, Louise acknowledged. Not that *she* would ever find him attractive. Far from it.

Liar, liar…a wickedly rebellious voice inside her head taunted. She must not think about that moment yesterday when, out of nowhere, she had suffered the awful, shaming indignity of a feeling as though she had been stripped of her defences, her body left nakedly vulnerable to an attack from its own sensuality. Logically it should have been impossible for her to have felt that searing, possessing jolt of female awareness, and all she could do now to comfort herself was to pretend to ignore it. It meant nothing, after all. But what if somehow her body…? *No.* She was not going to go down that route or start asking those questions. She needed to focus on the here and the now.

Of course the moment Caesar sat down next to her a waitress miraculously appeared, even though she had been sitting there without anyone coming anywhere near her for close on ten minutes prior to his arrival, and of course he ordered an espresso in contrast to her own *caffè latte.*

'I see that your son is having another tennis lesson this morning.'

'How do you know that?' There was no real reason for her to feel alarmed—no reason at all—but somehow she did.

'I happened to walk past the tennis courts as the children's club leaders arrived with their charges.'

'Well, hopefully I'll be able to go and watch him play myself if our meeting can be kept short.'

There was nothing wrong in her letting him know that she wanted this matter concluded. He might be lord of all he surveyed here on Sicily, but she wasn't going to bow and scrape to him even if she couldn't afford to actually offend him, she thought mutinously.

The waitress brought their coffee and handed Caesar Falconari his with so much deference that Louise half expected her to back away from him, bowing.

'As to that…there is a second matter I need to discuss with you in addition to your request for the burial of your grandparents' ashes.'

Another matter? She had been about to pick up her latte but now she left it where it was. Her heart-rate had picked up and was thumping heavily as alarm bells started ringing throughout her body.

'You see, just prior to your arrival here, and following on from your late grandfather's demise, I received a letter from his solicitors which he had written and given instructions to be posted to me following his death.'

'My grandfather wrote to *you*?'

Her throat had gone dry and her breath caught.

'Yes. It seems he had certain concerns for his great-grandson's welfare and his future. He felt he could not entrust you to deal with them, so he felt it necessary to write to me.'

Louise struggled to prevent her pent-up breath leaking away in an unsteady jerky movement that might betray her to him. It was true that her grandfather had had concerns about the growing anger and resentment Ollie was demonstrating towards her. He had even warned her that with so many families in their community knowing what they believed to be the story of her disgrace it wouldn't be long before Ollie was given that version of events at school. Children could be cruel to one another, both deliberately and accidentally, and Louise knew that Ollie already felt alienated enough from his peers because of his inability to name and claim a father, or even the family of his father, without the situation being made worse. However, as her grandfather had known, her hands had been tied.

It came as a dreadful shock to know that despite everything they had discussed, and despite the fact that she had believed her grandfather understood and accepted her decision, he had fallen victim to centuries of tradition and in his last weeks of life reverted to the Sicilian way of life she herself so much resented. Despite her love for him, and all that she owed him, after listening to Caesar Falconari's revelation it was impossible for her to stop her anger spilling over.

'He had no right to do that even if he did think he was acting in Ollie's best interests,' she said sharply. 'He knew how I felt about this whole Sicilian community thing of referring everything that is seen as some kind of problem to the community's *patronne* for judgement. It's totally archaic.'

'*Basta!* Enough! Your grandfather did not write to me as his *patronne*. He wrote to me because he claims that I am Oliver's father.'

The pain was immediate and intense, as though someone had ripped away the top layer of her skin, flooding her emotions, opening the locked gates to the past with all its shame and humiliation. She was eighteen again, shamed and disgraced, filled with confusing and only half-understood emotions that had come out of nowhere to change the path of her life for ever and marked her out in public as a fallen woman.

She could still see her father's face, with its expression of anger mixed with rejection as he'd looked at her, whilst Melinda had given her a gloating smile of triumph as she'd drawn her own daughters close to her and taken hold of her father's hand so that they formed a small close group that excluded her. Her grandfather's face had lost its colour, and her grandmother's hands had been trembling as she'd folded them together in her lap. No one seated in the popular café-bar in the small village square could have failed to hear the awful denunciation the headman of her grandparents' home village had made, labelling her as a young woman who had shamed her family by what she had done.

Automatically she'd turned to Caesar Falconari for support, but he had turned away from her, getting up from his seat to walk away, leaving her undefended and unloved—just as her father had done.

Hadn't she already been punished enough for her vulnerability and foolishness, without the added horror of *this*?

Louise winced, unable to stop that small betraying reaction to her memories of the past. She was still sensitive to his rejection. That should have been impossible. It *was* impossible, she assured herself. Her body was merely reacting to the memory of the pain he had once caused her, that was all. She needed to be here, in the present, not retreating to the past.

The very fact that he had spoken to her in Italian, with a harshly critical edge to his voice, was enough to warn Louise that Caesar was losing his patience with her—but why should she care about that when she had so much more to worry about? Oliver was her son—*hers*. He had nothing to do with Caesar, and if she had her way he never ever would. Even if Caesar *had* fathered him.

Caesar watched and saw the emotion she was struggling to suppress. The muscles in his own body tightened as he recognised that he would have preferred it had she immediately flown into a practised and fluent verbal assertion that her grandfather was right rather than accept that she was very obviously shocked, angry and afraid, and fighting not to show any of those feelings instead of laying claim to them. Hardly the action of a woman who wanted to claim him as the father of her child.

Louise shivered inwardly. How could her grandfather have done this to her? How could he have betrayed her like that? Shock, disbelief, pain, fear, and anger—Louise felt them all. And yet at the same time part of her could understand what might have motivated him.

She could so vividly remember that night—beaten down by the insistence of both her parents that she should have her pregnancy terminated, weeping in her grandmother's arms, feeling abandoned and afraid. She had finally told her grandparents what she had previously kept a secret: namely that, far from there being any number of young men to have potentially fathered her child, as the headman of the village had insinuated, there was only one who could have done so. And that one was no other than Caesar Falconari, Duca di Falconari, overlord of the vast wealth and estates on Sicily that had been her grandparents' birthplace.

Her grandparents had promised her that they would never betray that secret—but then they must have recognized, as she had known herself, that no one would ever believe her if she were to make such a claim. Especially not when Caesar himself… But, no. She was not going to go down that road. Not now and not ever. The bitterness of her past was best left buried beneath the new flesh she had grown over her old wounds. And besides she had Oliver to think of now.

She lifted her head and confronted Caesar. 'All you

need to know about Oliver is that he is my son and *only* my son.'

He had been afraid of this, Caesar admitted. His mouth compressing, he reached into his jacket pocket and produced the envelope containing her grandfather's letter, which he removed and placed on the table. As he did so the photographs her grandfather had enclosed with the letter fell onto the table.

Louise saw them immediately, her breath catching in a sharp drawn-in sound of rejection.

How different she looked in that old photograph taken that summer... They had all come here to Sicily, supposedly for a family holiday that would establish the new family dynamics that were being put in place following her parents' divorce. It had been Melinda's idea that she and her girls and Louise's father should join Louise and her grandparents on their visit to their original home, whilst Louise's mother was spending the summer with her 'friend' in Palm Springs.

Right from the start Louise had been in no doubt about Melinda's motives for suggesting the holiday. Melinda had wanted to reinforce yet again how unimportant she was to her father, and in contrast how important she and her own children were. That had been made obvious right from the start. And she had stupidly reacted exactly as Melinda had no doubt hoped she would, by doing everything she could to focus her father's attention on herself by the only means she knew—behaving so badly that he was *forced* to take notice of her.

Looking at herself in that photograph, it was hard for her not to cringe. She remembered that she had been attempting not just to emulate what she had naively perceived as Melinda's 'sexy' dressing, she had also attempted to outdo it. So she had translated the smooth sleekness of Melinda's dark brown hair into a black-dyed stringy mess that had clung to her scalp stiff with product. Melinda's favourite clingy short white jersey dress she had translated into a far too short, tight black jersey number, which she'd worn with stiletto heels instead of the pretty sandals of Melinda's choice. The tongue stud she had had put in in a mood of defiance at fifteen, long-gone now, had still been in place then, and black kohl surrounded her eyes. Her face was caked in far too much make-up.

On the face of it the photograph might depict an eighteen-year-old who looked far too sexually available, but the image looking back at her stabbed at Louise's heart. It wasn't just because she was looking at herself that she could see the vulnerability behind the overt sexuality. Anyone with her training and experience would be able to see the same thing. A caring father should surely also have seen it.

Louise looked again at the photograph. All that holiday she had deliberately worn clothes so provocative that it was hardly surprising she'd had virtually every boy in the village looking for easy sex, hanging around the villa they'd been renting. She'd looked cheap and available, and that was how she had been treated. Of course her grandparents had tried to suggest she wore something more discreet, and of course she had ignored them. She'd been very young for her age, despite her appearance— sent to an all-girls school, and just desperate to fit in and be accepted by the coterie of girls who mattered there. By changing her appearance she'd wanted to provoke her father, to force him to notice her. Of course he had not wanted anything to do with her, preferring instead to be with Melinda and her two pretty little girls.

What a fool she had been. And more than a fool.

'Quite a change,' Caesar couldn't help saying wryly when he saw her looking at the photograph her grandfather had included in his letter to jog his own memory about the identity of the young woman who had conceived what the dying man had claimed was *his* son. 'I wouldn't have recognised you.'

'I was eighteen and I wanted...'

'Male attention. Yes, I remember.'

Louise could feel her face beginning to burn.

'My *father's* attention...' she corrected him in a cool voice.

Was it the way she was looking at him or his own memories that stung with such unpalatable force? He had been twenty-two to her eighteen, newly in full control of his inheritance and free of the advisers who had previously guided him, and very much aware that his people were judging his ability to be the Duke they wanted— one who would preserve their traditions and way of life.

At the same time he'd been searching for a way to discreetly pursue his own plans for modernisation in the face of hostility to *any* kind of change amongst the older generation of headmen in charge of the villages. In particular the leader of the largest village, where Louise had been staying, had vetoed any idea of new developments— especially when it came to the role of women who, as far as he was concerned, must always be subservient to their menfolk and their family. That headman, Aldo Barado, had been able to marshal the support of many of the leaders from the other villages, which had led to Caesar feeling he had to tread very carefully and even make some concessions if he was to achieve his goals.

Whilst time and the growing insistence of the younger members of the community on modernising had helped to bring in many of Ceasar's plans, Aldo Barado remained unconvinced and still insisted on the old ways.

Louise's modern views, and her determination to be herself, had immediately caused Aldo Barado to be antagonistic towards her. He had come up to the *castello* within two days of Louise's arrival in the village to complain about the effect she was having on the young people, especially the young men, and even more especially on his only son who, despite the fact that he was engaged to be married in a match arranged and sanctioned by his father, had been openly pursuing Louise.

Of course Caesar had had no option other than to listen to the headman's demands that he do something about the situation and the girl who was openly flouting the rules of their society, and that was the reason and the only reason he had gone down to the village to introduce himself to her family—so that he could observe her behaviour and if necessary have a word with her father.

Only the minute he had set eyes on Louise any thought of remaining detached and ducal had been swept away, and he had known instantly, with gut-wrenching certainty, just why the village youths found her so compellingly attractive. Not even her atrocious hairstyle and choice of clothes had been able to dim the light of her extraordinary natural beauty. Those eyes, that skin, that softly pouting mouth that promised so much...

Caesar had been shocked by the force of his own response to her, and even more shocked by his inability to control that response. From the day he had been told of his parents' death, at six years old, he had developed emotional strategies to protect himself from the bewildering and often frightening aloneness he felt. He must be brave, he had been told. He must be strong. He must remember always that he was a Falconari and that it was his destiny and his duty to lead his people. He must put them, his family name and its history first. His own emotions didn't matter and must be controlled. He must always be a *duca* before he was a vulnerable human being.

After Aldo Barado's visit to complain about Louise he had, of course, tried to behave as he knew he should—even going to the extent of seeking out her father to express the headman's concern. But he knew now, after receiving Louise's grandfather's letter, that whilst he had listened to Aldo Barado, and to Louise's father and his wife-to-be, he had not made any attempt to listen to Louise herself. He had not looked beneath the surface. He had not seen what he should have seen.

Now, knowing how she had been rejected and treated by her father, he had to ask himself how much of that was down to him.

He looked at the photograph again. He had been so caught up in his own fear of the emotions she aroused in him that he had not seen what he could so plainly see now, and that was the unhappiness in the eyes of the girl in the photograph. Because he had not wanted to see it. It was guilt that was fuelling his anger now, he knew.

'And you expected to get your father's attention by going to bed with *me*?' he demanded caustically.

He was right. Of course he was right. Her behaviour had driven her father away, not brought them closer. Encouraged by the combined denunciations of both Aldo Barado and Melinda, her father, who had never been able to deal well with anything emotional, had turned on her, joining their chorus of criticism.

How naive she had been to expect that somehow Caesar would materialise at her side as her champion, her saviour, and tell them all that he loved her and he wasn't going to let anyone hurt her ever again. Caesar's very absence had told her all she needed to know about his real feelings for her, or the lack of them, even before the headman had told her father that he was acting on Caesar's instructions.

Now, when she looked back with the maturity and expertise she had acquired, she could see so clearly that what she had taken for Caesar's celebration of a shared love and a future for them, when he had abandoned his self-control to take them both to the heights of intimate physical desire, had in reality been a breaching of his defences by an unwanted desire for her that he had bitterly resented. Those precious moments held fast in his arms in the aftermath of their intimacy, which had filled her with such hope for the future and such joy, had filled *him* with a need to deny that what they had shared had any real meaning for him.

He might want to deceive himself about his own motivations, but she wasn't going to lie to him about the motives of that girl he had hurt so very badly.

Lifting her head, she gathered herself and let him hear the acid truth. 'Well, I certainly didn't go to bed with you so that I could be publicly humiliated by the headman of my grandparents' village whilst you remained aloof and arrogant in your *castello*! My father was furious with me for being, as he put it, "stupid enough to think that a man like Caesar could ever have wanted anything from you other than physical release." He said I'd brought shame on the whole family. My poor grandparents bore the worst of everything. Word spread quickly through the village, and if I wasn't actually stoned physically then I was certainly subject to critical glares and whispers. All because I'd been stupid enough to think I loved you and that you loved me.'

She paused for breath, savagely enjoying the release after keeping her pain locked away.

'Not that I'm sorry that you rejected me like that now. In fact I believe that you did me a favour. After all, you'd have dropped me anyway sooner or later, wouldn't you? A girl like me, with grandparents who were little more than your family's serfs, could *never* be good enough for *il duca*. That's what Aldo Barado told my grandparents when he did your dirty work for you and demanded that we leave.'

'Louise…' His throat felt dry, aching with the weight of the emotions crushing down on him. Only just like before he could not afford to give in to those emotions. Too much was at stake. Right or wrong, he couldn't turn his back on so many centuries of tradition.

He could apologise and try to explain. But to what purpose? In his letter Louise's grandfather had warned him of Louise's antagonism—not just towards him but also towards everything he represented. In her eyes they were already enemies, and Caesar knew that what he was going to tell her would only increase her hostility towards him.

Her grandfather had claimed in his letter that the intimacy he had shared with Louise had led to the birth of a child—a son. That should have been impossible, given that he had taken precautions. But if this child *was* his…

The heavy slam of his heart was giving away far too much and far more than he could afford to give away—even to himself.

She might not be able to defend her grandfather's behaviour in telling Caesar Falconari that Oliver was his son, but she could and would defend her own past, the victim she had in reality been, Louise decided grimly.

'When children grow up in an environment in which bad behaviour is rewarded with attention and good behaviour results in them being ignored, they tend to favour the bad behaviour. All they care about is the result they want,' she informed him.

And Caesar's love? Hadn't she wanted that as well? She had been too young, too immature to know properly what love—real love—meant. She speedily dismissed such a thought.

Louise was very much the educated professional in that statement, Caesar recognized.

'And you, of course, speak from personal experience?'

'Yes,' Louise agreed. She wasn't going to make excuses for her past—not to anyone. The love and forgiveness her grandparents had shown her had taught her so much, been such priceless gifts. She knew that Oliver's life would be the poorer for their loss.

'Is that why you trained as a specialist in family behaviour?'

'Yes.' There was no point in her denying it, after all. 'My own experiences, both bad and good, made me realise that I wanted to work in that field.'

'But despite that your own grandfather believed you were not dealing properly with your own son?'

It was too late now to regret that she hadn't been able to deal more positively with her grandfather's concerns about the way in which Oliver was reacting to his lack of a father. She herself believed that her son had certain distinctive character traits that could only have come down from the Falconaris—chief amongst them perhaps pride, and the hurt it caused to that pride that he did not have a father.

'Oliver has issues over the identity of his father,' she felt forced to admit. 'But, as my grandfather was perfectly well aware, I plan to put him in possession of the facts when I think he is old enough to deal with them.'

'And those facts are…'

'You know what they are. After all, Aldo Barado made them public enough. I came here to Sicily with my family. I went to bed with you. According to the headman of my grandparents' village I chased after and seduced his son. According to my father and Melinda I disgraced myself and shamed them by hanging around with boys who were quite obviously only after one thing, and then running after you. And they were right. I *did* humiliate and shame myself by going to bed with you. I wanted my father to sit up and take notice of me and—naively—I thought that being bedded by the most important man in the area was a good way to do that.'

She certainly wasn't going to tell him of the other reason she had pursued him so relentlessly. She could hardly bear to admit to herself even now the existence of that unfamiliar, shockingly sweet and half-frightening burgeoning of an emotional ache within her that had driven a genuine longing for physical intimacy with him.

For so long all Louise's emotional drive had been embedded in her quest for her father's love, so the sudden urgency of her feelings for Caesar had been her first true experience of the dangerous intensity of sexual desire. The strength of her instinctive impulse to reject that feeling had been almost as strong as the feeling itself. Initially she hadn't wanted anything to come between her and her goal. But over the days and weeks of their time in Sicily something had changed, and she had begun to see in Caesar, very dangerously, her future as the woman Caesar loved.

How naive she had been—and how vulnerable. And how blind to everything else. Brushing off the unwanted attentions of the headman's son as a mere nuisance, not realising how much her continued rejection of him had

damaged his pride, in a way that would demand retribution. That retribution had been the lies he had told about
her when he had claimed she had seduced him. Lies that
both his father, her family and Caesar himself had been
all too ready to believe.

From a professional point of view she could see how
much Caesar had been trapped in the demands imposed
on him by his culture. She was lucky. She had escaped
from its confining strictures. She was her own woman.
Although wasn't it the truth that she was still tied to the
past via her son? Like her, Ollie craved his father's love,
and his presence in his life.

Friends and colleagues had urged her to be open to
the prospect of a new relationship with a man who would
be a good role model for Ollie—a relationship based on
love and mutual respect—but no amount of professional
self-awareness or knowledge could banish her determination not to love again. For Ollie's sake as much as her
own. The raw truth was that she simply didn't trust herself not to love yet another man who would hurt her. She
had given everything she had to give to Caesar and he had
rejected her, allowed her to be humiliated and shamed.
Now, for her, the thought of sexual desire and of abandon-
ing herself to that desire was locked into a fear of giving
too much. Better not to allow *any* man into her life and
her bed than risk that happening.

'I used a condom on the night we had sex.'

She could hear Caesar even now denying the son he
had fathered, just as all those years ago he had denied
her. Well, she didn't care. Neither she nor Ollie needed
him in their lives—even if her grandfather had believed
otherwise. Her heart thumped heavily against her ribs.
If only her grandfather hadn't died. If only he was still
here to guard and guide Ollie's growth to adulthood. If

only she had never met Caesar. If only she had never gone to bed with him.

And never had Ollie? No…never.

'I am not the one who is claiming you as Oliver's father,' she pointed out to Caesar. 'That was my grandfather's decision.'

'But since he did make that claim…'

Louise stopped him. 'I suggest that you ignore it. Oliver has no need of an unwilling, doubtful father in his life who doesn't want him, and I have no intention of pursuing any kind of claim against you. That is not why I have come to Sicily. There is only one thing I want from you, and that is your authority for the burial of my grandparents' ashes in the churchyard of the church of Santa Maria.'

'But you do believe that the boy is mine?'

Why was he asking her such a question when she had just told him that she was prepared to let him off the hook?

'The only person I intend to discuss the matter of who might be Oliver's father is Oliver himself—once he is old enough to be able to deal with the circumstances surrounding his conception.'

'Surely it would be far easier simply for a DNA test to be done?'

'Why? Or do I need to ask? That could only be for your benefit and not Ollie's. You are obviously very sure that he isn't yours.'

'What I *am* very sure of is that I have no intention of allowing a child who might be mine—no matter how slender that possibility might be—to grow up thinking that I have abandoned him.'

His words shocked her—and all the more so because she could tell how heartfelt they were.

That cold feeling chilling right through her veins wasn't anger, Louise recognised, it was fear.

'And *I* have no intention of subjecting *my* son to a DNA test simply to put your mind at rest. If I were you I would simply accept that I have no intention of making any kind of claim on you as someone who might have fathered Oliver—and that means both emotionally and financially. Oliver is my son.'

'And according to his late great-grandfather he is also *my* son. If he is then I have a responsibility towards him that I cannot and will not ignore. At this stage there is no need for Oliver to be upset or worried in any way—a DNA test is a simple enough procedure to carry out without him even being aware that it *is* being carried out. A simple mouth swab is all that is required.'

'No.' She wasn't panicking. Not yet. But she was getting close to it, Louise recognised.

'You have told me how important it is to you that you carry out your grandparents' wishes with regard to their ashes. It is equally important to me that I know whether or not your son is also my son.'

He wasn't saying any more, but Louise knew exactly what he was getting at.

'That's blackmail,' she accused him. 'Do you think I would want as a father for my son a man who would threaten blackmail to get his own way?'

'I have every right to know if the boy is mine. Your grandfather obviously thought so, and he also obviously thought that the boy has a need for me in his life. He says as much in his letter. I do him the respect of believing that his claim on me on Oliver's behalf is not about money or status, but about a child's need to know its parentage. Can you sit there and honestly tell me, with your training, that you are prepared to deny your son that?'

'To deny him what? Being recognised as the bastard son of a man who allowed his mother to be publicly denounced and shamed? A man who is no doubt hoping right now that the test proves negative? A man who can never be anything to him other than someone who at best deigns to recognise him as his child without giving him anything that he really needs? Even if you *were* to recognise Oliver as your son, what can that bring him other than an even greater feeling of awareness than he already has that he is "less" than other children? There will always be those in a community, both here and at home in London, who look down on him because of his illegitimate status, just as there will be those who will never allow him to forget how he came to be conceived. I will *not* have my son pay for my sins.'

'You are making judgements that have no validity. If it turns out that Oliver is my son, then we shall discuss this matter again—and rationally—but for now I have to tell you that I intend to find out the truth about his parentage.'

He meant what he said, and he would somehow find a way to acquire the sample he would need, Louise suspected, true fear striking at her maternal emotions. Wouldn't it be far better for her to agree to provide the sample he was so obviously determined to have rather than run the risk of him trying to acquire it in a way that might upset Oliver?

Her voice heavy with reluctance and resistance, she said, 'If I agree to provide a DNA sample then in return I want your word that you will never approach my son with the results of the test—or indeed in any way at all without my permission and my presence.'

She was a very protective mother, Caesar recognised.

'I agree,' he confirmed. After all, the last thing he wanted to do was upset or damage the boy in any way.

Before she could continue to raise further objections he added smoothly, 'I shall arrange to have the necessary test kit delivered to you for return to me. Once I have the results…'

'Wouldn't it be simpler and easier for you to simply forget my grandfather's letter?' Louise suggested, in a last-ditch attempt to change his mind.

She'd promised herself that she wouldn't plead with him, but now she wasn't able to stop herself, she recognised helplessly, torn between anger against him and contempt for herself as she heard the slight tremor in her own voice.

'That's impossible,' Caesar told her.

CHAPTER THREE

'AND the only reason Billy won was because his father was there, watching us play and telling him what to do.'

Oliver had been complaining about losing his match with a fellow holidaymaker ever since Louise had picked him up from the children's club earlier in the day, and was still complaining about it now, as they had an early evening meal together.

Resisting the maternal impulse to comfort her plainly aggrieved son with a maternal cuddle—Oliver now considered himself far too old for maternal cuddles in public—Louise tried instead not to feel guilty about the small subterfuge she had been forced to practise to take the necessary DNA sample from her son, explaining away the procedure by saying that she thought he sounded slightly husky and she wanted to check his throat and make sure he wasn't coming down with one of the sore throats to which he was sometimes prone.

The sample, once taken, had been bagged up and handed over to the driver Caesar had sent to collect it. A man of Caesar's position and wealth would have his own ways of making sure that the test was dealt with speedily, Louise suspected. She, of course, already knew exactly what the test would reveal. Caesar *was* Oliver's father. She knew that beyond any kind of doubt. She knew it, but there was no way she had ever wanted Caesar himself to know it.

It was hard for her not to feel let down and even betrayed by the grandfather she had loved and respected so much, but she knew that he would have genuinely believed he was acting in Oliver's best interests. Her grandfather had been a man of his generation and upbringing—a man who'd believed that a father should take responsibility for his children.

All she had to do once the test confirmed her grandfather's claim was convince Caesar that she had no interest in claiming anything from him for her son, and thereby relieve him of the necessity to play any kind of role in Caesar's life. After all, her son was hardly a child he would want to own up to fathering, given what he thought of *her*—and, as she had already told him, there was no way she was going to allow Oliver ultimately to play second fiddle to Caesar's legitimate children.

Louise frowned to herself. She was rather surprised that, given his title and the traditions that went with it, Caesar wasn't already married with children. He was bound to want an heir. His title, like his land and his wealth, had descended in an unbroken line from father to son for over a thousand years. There was no way that an arrogant man like Caesar was going to be the one to break that tradition. Not that she cared about that. Her concern and anxiety were for Oliver.

After she had left Caesar and the coffee shop she had gone to collect Oliver to take him for lunch, arriving just as his match had ended so that she'd been in time to see the way Oliver had been trying to gain the attention and the praise of the father of the boy with whom he had been playing. Witnessing the anger and the frustration on her son's face had torn at her maternal heart as nothing else

could. She could see so much of her own fear and humiliation in Oliver's behaviour, and she understood only too
well what Oliver was going through.

When Billy's father had walked off with his own son
she'd had to fight back her desire to run to Oliver and
give him the praise and the attention he so obviously
wanted, but she had stopped herself because she knew
perfectly well that it was a *man's* attention Oliver wanted,
not a mother's.

Tomorrow she was taking Oliver to a water park for
the day; she felt guilty about the fact that she'd had to
give so much time to trying to sort out the burial of her
grandparents' ashes, even though that was the prime purpose of their visit.

There must be other single parents here in the hotel
with their children, but so far she hadn't seen any. In
fact the hotel, which she'd chosen because of its well-
recommended children's facilities, seemed to be filled
with happy couples and their equally happy children.

Louise repressed a small sigh as Oliver reached for his
games console, warning him with a shake of her head,
'Not until after we've finished dinner, please, Ollie. You
know the rules.'

'Everyone else is using theirs. That Billy and his dad
are *both* playing on his.'

Louise sighed again and looked across to where father
and son had their heads close together over the small
screen.

In the *castello* which had first been built by his ancestors
to guard the land they had been granted as the spoils of
war, and which had been extended and renovated many,
many times over the centuries, until it had become the
magnificently fronted and redesigned architectural work

of art that it was today, Caesar stood looking down the length of the long gallery at its portraits of his ancestors. A portrait of every Duca di Falconari since the first had been commissioned, and then, from the fourteen-hundreds onwards, family groups as well, depicting not just the *ducas* but also their duchesses and their children—their heirs, in their court finery, the second sons in cardinal's hats—all of them painted to portray the enduring power of the Falconari name.

No Falconari had ever failed to produce a son—a legitimate heir—to carry on the name after him. His own father had married again late in life to an equally blue-blooded member of a distant branch of the family from Rome to produce Caesar himself. Both his parents had been killed in a sailing accident when he was six but throughout his childhood it had been impressed on Caesar how important it was that he too married and produced the next generation of Falconaris.

'It is our duty to our people and to our name,' his father had always told him.

He was thirty-one. He knew that amongst the older generation of elders and village headmen the fact that he had not fulfilled that duty was a matter of increasing concern. None of them would understand his revulsion against himself and his own sexuality which he had felt in the aftermath of his relationship with Louise. His fear of losing his self-control again, as he had done with her, had forced him to remain celibate for many, many months after she had gone. But then, when he had eventually decided that he had to test his own strength of will against his sexuality, he had received another shock.

He had discovered that he was perfectly capable of remaining in control of himself and his responses even with the most beautiful and sensual of women. His ability to control his life had been restored. He had told himself that he was delighted. He had reminded himself that he didn't want to experience that sense of loss of self, of merging so completely with another person that they were no longer two separate human beings but one indivisible whole, and that had certainly been the truth. Wasn't it another truth, though, that for him the intimacy of sex had lost its savour and become an empty pleasure that couldn't satisfy or stem the ache he had locked away deep within himself?

An ache which he had already felt intensifying just because of Louise's presence...

It was because of Louise that he had held off from marriage. Because he had known...

What? That no woman could ever touch his emotions or arouse his desire as she had done?

He had come to the last portrait—of himself when he had come of age. He had been twenty-one then. For the last six years, thanks to an unexpected and cruel blow of fate, he had had to live with the fact that he was destined to be the last of his line. Until, that was, he had received Louise's grandfather's letter, informing him that *he* was the father of her child and that he had a son.

Caesar could feel the heavy slamming thud of his own heartbeat and the overwhelming tide of fierce emotion it brought with it. His child—flesh of his flesh—linked to him by a bond so strong that the very thought of not loving or wanting him was inconceivable. He would never be able to understand what had motivated Louise's father to reject and hurt her as he had done. Such behaviour was the antithesis of everything he himself believed fatherhood should be—everything his fathering of Oliver would be if the boy did prove to be his. And he *wanted* Oliver to be his. Caesar knew that. He wanted him to be his with an intensity that went above and beyond mere practicality and duty. From the minute he had read Louise's grandfather's letter he had been filled with a maelstrom of emotions so fiercely intense that now, deep within himself, the inner core of everything that he was was insisting to him that, no matter what precautions he might have taken to deny her, the overwhelming surge of passion they had shared had somehow allowed nature to have its way.

Yet Louise was making it plain that she did not want him to be involved in his son's life.

Louise.

He could remember very well the afternoon he had first met her, walking on her own along the dusty road that led from the village to the *castello*, her head bare, her too-tight clothes revealing the sensual shape of her body, her eyes alive with wariness and intelligence. Her whole manner had been one of rebellious defiance against the old order of things and those who imposed it. She had been seen drinking beer from a bottle, laughing and dancing in the village square, encouraging the village's young men to defy their parents.

She'd looked at him with such a clear-eyed assessing gaze that he had initially been amused by her boldness and then intrigued by Louise herself. No one, least of all a village girl, looked him directly in the eye like that.

He had asked her where she was going, and she had tossed her mane of darkly dyed hair and told him that there was nowhere to go and she couldn't wait to get back to London. He had asked her how she would have been spending her time had she been in London, and she had surprised him by answering that she would have been visiting the National Portrait Gallery and preparing herself for the art degree she planned to start in the autumn term.

He had known even at that early stage exactly what kind of effect she was having on him. A twenty-two-year-old male's body didn't possess any subtlety. It knew what it wanted. And his had certainly let him know that it wanted her. Wanted her, but couldn't possibly get involved with her. In London she might be a city girl, with all that meant, but here on Sicily she was a member of the community for which he was responsible. And yet even knowing that he had still invited her to go back to the *castello* with him, so that she could view his own portrait gallery.

She had blushed then, he remembered, suddenly looking so sweetly feminine and uncertain that he had immediately wanted to protect her.

'You will come to no harm,' he had assured her. 'You have my word on that.'

'The word of a *duca* and therefore of far more value than the word of a mere mortal?' she had mocked him, with one of those lightning changes of response that had always managed to catch him off guard.

To have her taunting him like that, as though she was the one who was in control, had piqued him enough to have him exchanging the kind of sensually charged banter with her that, whilst perfectly acceptable, still held an erotic edge to it. And she had responded in kind, so that they had occupied their walk back to the *castello* like two expert duellists engaged in a verbal swordfight.

He had shown her the portrait gallery, and she had swiftly picked out those portraits painted by the great masters, surprising him by admiring his own Lucian Freud portrait and commenting that she was surprised that he had chosen such a modern and often controversial painter.

'I bet Aldo Barado doesn't like it,' she had challenged

him, and of course he had been forced to agree that she was right.

'He is a good man,' he had said in defence of the head-man. 'I value his advice and his knowledge.'

'And his desire to keep his people locked into out-of-date customs—especially when those people are female? Do you value that as well?' she had demanded.

'He has his pride, and I would never want to damage that, but I can see that there are changes that need to be made—changes that I want and plan to make.'

Even now it still gave him a sharp shock of disbelief that he should have been able to confide in her so easily and so quickly. Even then there had been something about her that said she had an understanding of and a compassion for human nature that outweighed her years. Her choice of career had proved that.

It had been inevitable right from the start that he would take her to bed. Was it equally inevitable that she should have conceived his child?

His heart thudded into his ribs with truly ferocious blows.

It was simply because she had come to bed early that she couldn't sleep, Louise assured herself as she stood on the balcony of the twin room she was sharing with Oliver, who was fast asleep in his own bed.

The gardens beyond the hotel sparkled with lights, in the trees and around the pools. Somewhere on the complex music was playing. From her balcony she could see couples strolling arm in arm. Couples. That was something that could never happen for her—being part of a couple. She'd always be far too afraid of somehow regressing to the needy, self-damaging girl she had been, and repeating her old mistakes. More important than that, though, was Oliver. She would never take the risk of introducing into their lives a man who might damage her son by letting either of them down.

Down on the ground below her a small group of teenagers passed by, reminding her of how *she* had been the last time she had come to Sicily. A teenager who had been punished so cruelly and so publicly. Louise could feel herself compressing her muscles against the savage bite of memories she didn't want resurrected. Some things never stopped inflicting pain, no matter how much thick skin one tried to grow over the wound.

It had been midway through their holiday. Her father hadn't spoken to her for three days because he was ashamed of her—both of how she looked and how she behaved.

Melinda, of course, had been looking like the cat who had got the cream, constantly drawing attention to Louise's failings whilst making sure that her father saw how enchantingly pretty and well behaved her own daughters were in contrast. Pretty, self-confident little girls, who weren't at all hesitant about begging sweetly for ice cream.

Since Melinda had come into her father's life there had been a constant and—on Louise's part—increasingly desperate war between them to win his loyalty. A war which Louise had felt deep down inside herself she was destined to lose—until she had met Caesar on the fateful solitary walk she had taken to escape from Aldo Barado's son Pietro's increasingly unpleasant attentions. She'd done nothing to encourage him. At least not in her own book. Yes, she'd initially enjoyed the fuss the local boys had made of her, feeling very grown up and streetwise compared with the village girls who had such cloistered lives. Yes, she'd broken an unwritten local rule by drinking beer in the village bar in the company of those boys, but she had never, *ever* given Pietro the kind of encouragement he claimed she had given him.

It was no exaggeration to say that meeting Caesar, realising who he was and accepting his invitation to the *castello*, had changed the whole course of her life. Not that she had guessed how radical that change would be on that first day. She had heard her grandparents talking about him, and knew the high regard, almost awe, with which he was revered, and had seized on what she had seen as an opportunity to outmanoeuvre Melinda via a relationship with Caesar. At eighteen she had been too naive to reason any further than that. It had been enough that Caesar had shown an interest in her.

By the time she had realised that being with Caesar was more important to her than winning her father's approval it had been too late for her to pull back. She'd been in love with Caesar. When he'd visited the village she had made sure that she was there—even if that meant she had to frequent the bar and endure the unwanted attentions of the headman's son to make sure she would bring herself to Caesar's attention. She had hung on his every word, ignoring Pietro's anger when the gang of boys who hung around with him made fun of him because he was being supplanted in her affections by their *Duca*.

'You are a fool,' Pietro had spat at her furiously. 'He is not really interested in you! How could he be? He is a *duca*.'

It wasn't any more than she had already told herself, but his unkind words had stung, making her determined to prove him and everyone else wrong. She hadn't told him about those private 'accidental' meetings, when she had walked close to the *castello*, glancing up at the windows which Caesar had told her belonged to his private

suite of rooms, and her persistence had been rewarded
by Caesar's appearance. Their walks together, the conversation they had shared, had been so precious to her.
Caesar hadn't laughed at her as others did.

It had only been a matter of a few very small steps
for a girl of her emotional vulnerability to start creating inside her head a fairytale situation in which Caesar
returned her love, and by doing so set her not just on a
duchess's throne but also a shining, happy pedestal from
which she could bask in the admiration and the approval
of her father. However, to her disappointment, despite the
time they'd been spending together, Caesar had made no
attempt to take their relationship any further. Instead of
taking up her silent invitation he'd backed off from her—
even if on one particularly hot, sultry afternoon towards
the end of the holiday he had been so obviously furiously
angry at finding her in the village bar with Pietro that
she had been sure he was jealous.

'You are risking your reputation with your behaviour,'
he had told her when she had accused him of jealousy
later. 'It is that which concerns me on your behalf.'

'What about Pietro?' she had challenged him. 'Isn't
he also risking *his* reputation?'

'It is different for a man—at least here in this part of
the world,' had been his answer.

'Well, it shouldn't be. Because it isn't fair,' she had told
him, with all her own feelings about her relationship with
her father intensifying her vulnerable emotions.

Instead of giving vent to her feelings about the un-
fairness of the community's customs she should have
paid more attention to his warning on a personal level,
Louise acknowledged. It was too late for such regrets
now, though. Far, far too late.

She had been such a fool, seeing in Caesar's behaviour towards her what she had wanted to see instead of reality. She had convinced herself that Caesar loved her as passionately as she had him. Naively, even laughably, she had completely ignored the barriers between them, convinced that all that mattered was their feelings for one another, even though Caesar had given her no indication whatsoever that he felt the same way as her.

The night Oliver had been conceived she had been desperate to see him. He'd been away from the village on business, and when she'd heard that he had returned her need to be with him had been so great that nothing could have stopped her from doing what she had done. They were destined to be together—she had known it. Their fates, their futures would be entwined as surely as those of Romeo and Juliet.

She'd hoped that Caesar would come down to the village, and when he hadn't, fuelled by her longing to be with him, she'd claimed a headache and pretended to go to bed. Instead she'd gone to the *castello*, sneaking in through the open kitchen door and finding her way to Caesar's room.

He had been busy working on his computer when she'd walked in, a look of shock stilling his face when he'd seen her. He'd got up from his chair, but when she'd run towards him he had fended her off, demanding tersely, 'Louise, what are you doing here? You shouldn't be here.'

Hardly the words of a devoted lover. But she'd been too wrought up and possessed by her own emotions to pay any heed to them. Caesar loved and wanted her, she knew he did, and now she was going to show him how much she loved and wanted him. It had made her feel so grown up to take control of the situation like that. To be the one to drive their relationship forward to the intimate closeness that they both wanted.

'I had to come,' she'd told him. 'I want to be with you so much. I want *you* so much, Caesar,' she'd emphasized, closing the door and then walking towards him, removing her jacket as she did so, keeping her gaze fixed on his face as she mimicked a scene from a film she'd seen in London during which the actress slowly removed her clothes as she walked towards the hero.

It hadn't take her long to get down to her underwear. She hadn't been wearing very much—just a simple cotton dress under her denim jacket. Even her much prized Doc Marten boots had been exchanged for a pair of slip-on flat shoes so that she could step out of them easily. She'd stretched behind herself to unfasten her bra, and then stopped to look right at him and beg huskily, 'You do it, Caesar. You unfasten it,' before hurling herself towards him.

He'd caught hold of her immediately, as she'd known he would. What she *hadn't* known, though—until then—was how safe it felt to be in his arms, as well as how exciting. Safety and excitement—opposites. And yet right then in Caesar's arms they had seemed to fit together perfectly—just as she and Caesar would also fit together perfectly when he made her his.

She'd kissed the side of his jaw, overwhelmed by what being so close to him was doing to her. It had been a clumsy, inexperienced kiss, and it had thrilled and shocked her when she'd felt the stubble of his skin beneath the softness of her parted lips. He had felt so male, so alien and dangerous, and yet at the same time so safe—because he was hers, because he loved her.

Believing that had given her the courage to demand, 'Kiss me, Caesar, kiss me now. *Now*,' she had repeated on a soft moan as she clutched at his arms and lifted her mouth towards his.

He'd tried to deny her, to push her away, insisting, 'This can't happen, Louise. We both know that. It must not happen.'

Louise hadn't wanted to listen. She'd been beyond listening, she acknowledged now. She'd heard other girls talking about how it felt to be turned on by a boy, but this was the first time she'd experienced it.

She'd kissed him again but this time as he'd tried to wrench her arms from around his neck they'd fallen together onto the bed, and then she'd felt it—the hard evidence of his arousal.

She'd trembled violently with that knowledge and pressed herself closer to him, ignoring his savage, '*No, this must not happen.*'

Louise stared out into the darkness. It made her feel physically sick now to acknowledge how badly and self destructively she'd behaved. With maturity she could accept that within a man pushed hard enough a certain chain reaction could be activated, transmuting anger into a physical male desire that had nothing to do with any kind of tender emotion for the woman involved.

His hands had locked round her wrists and he'd held her beneath him. His thumb pads, she remembered, had found the racing pulse-points beneath her skin. Totally ill-equipped to understand or handle her own female sensuality, she had cried out in shock as the warmth of his touch caused a weakening longing to surge through her body. That was when it had happened. That was when she had lost all thought of why she was there and had only been able to think about what being so intimately close to him was doing to her. With one heartbeat she had slipped from one world to another, changed for ever by that happening. All her caution had left her, all sense of anything other than what was happening. Like the opening of a floodgate she had started to tell him how much she wanted him, how much he aroused her, how much she loved him, scattering kisses over his face and throat, clinging to him, pleading with him.

If she was trembling now, remembering that moment, then it was because of the night air against the bare flesh of her arms—nothing more. She wanted to go back inside and escape the memories of what it had meant to lie naked in a man's arms in the scented warmth of the Sicilian night. Behind her the safety of her hotel room would no doubt be smelly with the reality of Ollie's trainers, its silence broken not by the accelerated breathing of two people possessed by mutual sexual need but by those little noises Ollie was still young enough to make in his sleep. She needed that reality, but the memories linking her to the past, once unleashed, were too strong for her to deny. What had happened that fateful night couldn't be denied. After all Oliver himself was the living, breathing evidence of Caesar's possession of her.

From the unshuttered windows of Caesar's bedroom she had been able to see outlined against the star-studded moonlit sky the distant mountains, and the white-hot heat running through her veins had been every bit as dangerous as Mount Etna's lava flow.

The fierce grind of Caesar's lower body into her own, so compulsively male, so previously unknown and yet somehow at the same time immediately recognised by her own flesh, the harsh possession of his kiss, her first true kiss—everything about their intimacy had had a dark magic about it that she had been powerless to resist. There in that Caesar-scented night-dark room she had come of age as a woman, and her body had gloried in that happening.

There was no point in trying to convince herself now

that the thrill she had felt then had been solely engendered by the triumph she had felt in arousing Caesar's desire, because she and her body both knew the truth. The thrill she had felt, the delight and the desire she had felt, had sprung from a need within herself that she had actively encouraged and celebrated—from the taut sensitivity of her nipples, where they'd rubbed against the hair-darkened masculinity of the chest Caesar had bared for her touch, to the liquid heat of female desire that had pounded so fiercely within her sex. She had wanted him, and her need to have him answer that wanting had been as unstoppable as her need to breathe.

There was no point telling herself that it was merely the wine she had drunk earlier that evening that had melted away her inhibitions. She knew that wasn't true. There in Caesar's bed, in Caesar's arms, her need for his possession had surely sprung from an embedded age-old female pre-conditioning to mate with the man who was the strongest of his tribe and whose genes would most benefit the child he might give her.

Not that she had analysed her reaction like that then, of course. Then she had simply told herself that being there in Caesar's arms, knowing that he wanted her, was the fulfilment of her ultimate fantasy and would prove she was worthy of another's love.

There'd certainly been no holding back on her part when Caesar had invited her to touch him intimately, placing her hand over the thick, pulsing heat of his erection.

Her heart slammed into her chest wall, her hand trembling as she fought against the intensity of the physical memory invading her body and her senses. It surely shouldn't be possible to have reconstructed that exact moment and those feelings—not when she had buried those memories so deeply. Sicily—it was Sicily and her blood heritage that was reviving them. That and the knowledge of what her grandfather had done, and the far more dangerous realities his letter had unleashed.

She tried to redirect her thoughts, but it was no use. They were as out of her control as her body had been that night, commanded by a far greater authority.

She could still remember how her heart had raced and pounded at the feel of his flesh beneath her touch, before settling into a heavy, fast rhythm that had matched the pulse within his sex and then within her own as it had taken up the beat his had set. She had been wet and ready when his fingers had parted her sex, slippery with the juices of desire and excitement, and her eyes had opened wide, her body arcing in disbelief before melting into shuddering climax beneath his skilled touch against her clitoris.

How naive she had been. Wholly caught up in her feelings of loss and abandonment, at eighteen she had had no real knowledge at all of her own sexuality. Technically she had known what happened, but that hadn't prepared her for the reality of the hot gush of pleasure that had engulfed her, causing her to cry out Caesar's name and cling helplessly to him as her body rode its first climactic storm.

To have Caesar enter her then, whilst her flesh was still quivering with sensuality, still swollen with pleasure, could have done nothing other than result in another shocking surge of response to the movement of his flesh within her own.

This time her orgasm had been even more intense, causing her to rake her fingernails against Caesar's flesh. In answer he had driven even more deeply within her, and her muscles had fastened around him, clinging to him as though reluctant to let him go, she remembered—how could she forget? Exhausted by the intensity of her experience she had lain still in Caesar's arms, her love for him filling her heart. How ridiculous she had been, thinking that because Caesar was still holding her it meant that he loved her. She wouldn't stay with him all night, though, she had decided. The intimacy they had shared was too precious and too private to be pawed over by other people, as it would be if her bed was found to be unslept in the morning. She'd wanted Caesar to be the one who announced their relationship to her family—and especially to her father. She'd been able to see them, standing hand in hand whilst he drew her closer and told her family proudly that he loved her.

'I must go,' she'd whispered to Caesar.

'Yes,' he had agreed. 'I think you must.'

If she had been disappointed that he didn't share with her the shower he had invited her to take before she left, then she'd made herself hide that disappointment. After all there would be other occasions for them to share such intimacy—many of them now that they were lovers.

Caesar, she remembered, had accompanied her back to the road—not because he had wanted to be with her, Louise thought grimly now. No, what he had wanted was to make sure she left the *castello*.

Walking the short distance from the *castello* to the villa where they'd been staying, all she had been able to think about was seeing Caesar again. For the first time in her life someone other than her father had filled her thoughts. For the first time in her life someone had shown how important she was to them. For the first time in her life there was someone who would put her first. All her dreams had come true. Caesar loved her. Tonight had proved that.

Things hadn't worked out as she had expected.

There had been no sign of Caesar the following day, or the days that followed it. No word. Nothing. And then she'd learned that Caesar had left the *castello* to fly to Rome, and that he would be remaining there for over a month attending to family business.

At first she hadn't been able to take it in. There had to be some mistake. Caesar must have intended to see her and tell her personally that he was leaving. He must have wanted to speak with her father and make their relationship public. At the very least he must surely have left her a letter or a message.

She'd been beside herself with disbelief, anxiety and the pain of missing him. She had even tried to persuade her family to extend their holiday. And that had been when the reality of what Caesar actually felt about her was revealed to her in the most cruel and humiliating way possible.

Her grandparents had been open to the idea of them prolonging their visit, and her grandfather had even gone to see the owner of the rented villa to discuss extending their stay. However, before the villa's owner had come back to him with his answer, the family had received a visit from Aldo Barado during which he had said there was no way the village wanted the family to extend their visit and that in fact they were eager to be rid of them because of the shame they had brought on themselves and the village via Louise's behaviour.

'You are not welcome here any longer,' he had said angrily, before turning to Louise's father to accuse him savagely, 'No father in the village, or indeed in Sicily, would permit his daughter to behave as you have allowed yours to. She shames us all with her behaviour, but most of all she shames you—her father. You have turned away from your duty and she has set about offering herself to the young men of our village—no doubt hoping to trap one of them into marriage.'

He had turned to her then, Louise remembered, his back to her family, his eyes cold with anger as he had told her, 'Fortunately those involved have sought and listened to my counsel. There will be no future opportunities for your daughter to pursue them. In future this village will no longer recognise you as members of its community.'

Still unable to take in what was happening, Louise had turned after him as he had strode off, catching hold of his sleeve in an attempt to stop him. He had pulled away from her as though her touch contaminated him, but she had ignored that, insisting, 'Caesar would never have allowed this to happen. He loves me.'

'Our *Duca* is in Rome and will remain there until you have gone—on my advice after he confessed to me his foolishness. As for him loving you? Do you *really* think that any decent man, never mind one so exalted, and with the responsibilities that our *Duca* carries, would ever love a woman like you?'

'He told you about…about us?' That had been all she was capable of saying as shock and anguish gripped her.

'Of course he told me.'

With that he had walked away, leaving her with no option other than to return to her family. Her father had been furious with her, pacing the tiled floor of the terrace as he gave vent to his feelings. He was a man who didn't like being criticised by anyone over anything, and he had held nothing back as he had accused her of being involved in something that proved all over again how undeserving she was of being his daughter.

'When I think of the time and money I have lavished on you—and this is how you repay me, putting me in a position where I have to listen to the criticism of a man who is little better than a goatherder. My God, if this ever got out to anyone at the university I'd become a complete laughing stock—and all because of you.'

'Darling, I did warn you that you were spoiling her,' Melinda had put in with a *faux* tender smile. 'She really doesn't deserve to have such a wonderful father. I've said so over and over again.'

It had been the hurt she'd seen in her grandparents' eyes that had caused her the most pain.

She shouldn't have come back here, but what choice did she really have? Making sure they had the final resting place they had wanted was far more important to her than her own feelings. She had to admit, though, that she had been taken off guard by her grandfather's actions in writing to Caesar, on what would have virtually been his deathbed, to tell him about Oliver.

Despite the warmth of the night Louise folded her arms around her body as though to protect it from the cold—but this cold was an inner cold, not an outer one, an icy chill that came from knowing that potentially Caesar had power over her.

Once again her thoughts were drawn back to the past. After the headman had left and her father had had his say he and Melinda had stopped speaking to her, as though they could hardly bear to look at her. Only her grandparents, obviously distressed by the whole awful experience, had continued to speak to her—even though she'd seen how shocked and upset they were. She'd been shocked and upset herself, of course, and brutally forced to recognise what a fantasy world she'd been inhabiting. She'd tried to talk to her father but he'd cut her off, telling her furiously that he no longer wanted her in his life.

The return trip to the airport had been a nightmare.

As they'd driven through the village on their way back to the airport those villagers who had been in the town square had turned away from the car, and some of the young men had even thrown stones at it. Her father had been furious with her, but it was the memory of the tears in her grandfather's eyes that still hurt her the most.

She wasn't eighteen any more, Louise reminded herself. She was nearly twenty-eight, and a highly qualified professional in her field, who had to deal daily with problems within relationships and emotionally driven people who'd had experiences that were far, far worse than her own. The problems of her past were not hers alone. Others had shared in their creation.

Her main responsibility now was doing what was best for Oliver. She might remain trapped in the present, yes, because of the events of the past, but she did not have to be trapped within her own pain. She had been foolish in creating her fantasy around Caesar, and she had paid for that folly and come through the trauma of it. Caesar, she suspected, because of his position and the deference accorded to him, would never experience the stripping-down of his personality to reveal to him its inherent flaws; he had never been humiliated, never been humbled, never been told that he was cruel—and that, in her professional opinion, was his loss. He had denied her and now he wanted to claim his son. The idea filled her with terror. She would never allow anyone, least of all Caesar, to hurt and humiliate Oliver the way she had been hurt.

She wished passionately that it wasn't necessary for her to have to have Caesar's permission for the interment of her grandparents' ashes, but she wasn't going to give up just because of the past. She was determined to repay the debt she owed them. And if Caesar's price for that was Oliver's DNA test…? Well, she would be ready to do battle for her son…and for her very soul.

CHAPTER FOUR

His title and standing on the island opened many doors, Caesar acknowledged as the manager in charge of the children's club at the hotel escorted him onto the tennis court where Oliver had just finished playing. Caesar had told him that he was thinking of enrolling his cousin's sons for lessons when they arrived later in the week for their annual summer visit. It need not be a lie. His cousin had mentioned that it was becoming increasingly difficult to keep her teenage sons fully occupied.

Oliver, who was focused on his computer game, only looked up briefly when Caesar's shadow fell across his screen.

Oliver's colouring wasn't only entirely Sicilian—olive-coloured skin, a mop of dark curls—it was also entirely Falconari, Caesar recognised as the boy's eyes registered wary hesitation at the approach of a stranger.

In Caesar's jacket pocket were the results of the DNA test, and they were beyond doubt. They showed absolutely clearly that Oliver was his son. Looking at him now, Caesar was caught off guard by the ferocity and surging intensity of the father-to-son connection he felt towards him. It was so strong that it was almost as though an actual cord somehow connected them. Immediately he wanted to go to Oliver and take hold of him, lay claim to him, mark him by his touch as his own.

The power and the unexpectedness of the personal nature of the emotions gripping him almost stopped him mid-stride. He'd already known what it would mean to him as the Duca di Falconari to know that Oliver was his son, but this feeling went far beyond that and was very personal.

Thankfully, though, he did have some experience of boys around Oliver's age through his contact with his cousin's sons, so he held back and merely remarked conversationally, 'You played well.'

'You were watching me?'

With those words the look Oliver was giving him and his wariness dropped away, to be replaced with a pleasure that underlined more clearly than anything else could have done the issues his great-grandfather had raised in his letter:

> The boy needs his father in his life. Louise is a good mother—she loves him and protects him—but the unhappiness she experienced with her own father has cast a long shadow, and that shadow falls on Oliver as well. He needs the genuine love and presence in his life of his father. I can see the same craving in him that Louise herself suffered. You are his father. You have a duty to him that I believe your honour will oblige you to meet.
> This isn't about money. Louise has a good job, and I know she would refuse to take any kind of financial help from you.

From what he had seen so far of Louise, Caesar doubted that she would be willing to take *anything* from him.

He had been relieved, or so he had told himself, when he had returned from Rome to find her gone—even if his twenty-two-year-old's pride *was* still stinging from being accosted by the village headman. Especially as, when he'd initially heard the brief knock on his bedroom door, he'd thought it was Louise returning to him. Knowing that he had felt a leap of joy added to the weight of his guilt and his confusion about his inability to control his reaction to Louise, and had been enough to make him feel obliged to listen whilst the headman warned him that he had seen Louise leaving the *castello*. He'd guessed what had happened and told him that if Caesar wanted to prove he was fit to wear his ancestors' noble shoes, that he was aware of his duty to his people, then he could have nothing more to do with Louise.

'That just isn't possible,' Caesar had told him. 'Her family are staying here. They are part of our extended community. It is expected that I make them welcome.'

And Louise? He had wanted to make *her* welcome too—in his bed. And in his heart…? How torn he had been between the raging desire that she had released and his awareness of the customs of his people. But his desire for Louise was something he had to control and deny, he had warned himself. Just as he had controlled and denied any public display of the shock and grief he had felt at the loss of his parents. It was not seemly for a Falconari to allow himself to be controlled by his emotions, so he'd absented himself until his fear that his ability to control his emotions had been breached for ever had gone.

Was it seemly for a Falconari to take the coward's way out? What was the point of asking himself these questions? There was no point—just as there was no point in allowing himself to remember the emotional agony he had felt in Rome, the sleepless nights, his desire to find Louise… Another example of her ability to breach his self-control—just like the letter he had eventually sent her, asking for forgiveness. A letter to which she had never replied. Not even though by then she must have known she was carrying his child.

He looked down into Oliver's eyes. Exactly the same colour and shape as his own. His heart pounded uncontrollably.

'How are you liking Sicily?' he asked.

'It's much better than home 'cos it's warm. I hate the cold. My great-grandparents were Sicilian. My mum's brought their ashes here to get them buried.'

Caesar nodded his head.

Another boy was coming towards them, swinging a racquet and accompanied by a man who Caesar guessed must be his father.

'Hi, Oliver.' The man smiled. 'I see you've got your dad with you now.'

Caesar waited for Oliver to deny their relationship, but instead, almost instinctively, he moved closer to him, so that Caesar could put his hand on Oliver's shoulder in much the same way the other man was doing with his son.

Oliver's bones beneath his tee shirt felt thin and young, vulnerable and very precious. So *this* was how it felt to have a child…a son…

And that was how Louise saw them as she came to collect Oliver, her pace quickening along with the anxious, angry too-fast beat of her heart, until both were racing as she almost ran up behind Oliver, reaching out to wrench him out of Caesar's hold.

They turned towards her at the same time, father and

son, the truth stamped so indelibly on both sets of features that the shock of it sent her heart into a flurry of frightened hammer-blows. Even worse was seeing the way in which Oliver immediately moved closer to Caesar when she tried to part them.

Caesar still had one hand on Oliver's shoulder, and now he lifted the other hand to cover hers where she'd grabbed Oliver's arm. Immediately a sensation of physical danger sent a trail of fiery sparks burning through her veins. Her whole body was reacting so frantically and fearfully to Caesar's touch that she was forced to ask herself if her panic was on Oliver's account or on her own. The awareness that was pulsing through her right now wasn't just maternal anxiety and she knew it. It was something else. Something very different. Different and totally unwanted. But not totally unfamiliar.

It was like lightning coming out of nowhere to tear apart the sky, its brilliance throwing piercingly sharp light into previously hidden places. Louise could feel the impact of the blow on her memory breaking apart the locks she had put on it. Wasn't it the unpalatable truth that this was the way Caesar had made her feel all those years ago? The very thought made her shudder with horror and self-loathing. How could her body possibly find Caesar attractive either now? He had humiliated her, shamed her, treated her with contempt.

She tried to snatch her hand from beneath his but he refused to let her go, so that she was forced to stand there whilst the three of them completed a small intimate circle.

'I was just on my way to look for you,' Caesar told her. 'We have a great deal to discuss.'

'The only thing I want to discuss with you is the interment of my grandparents' ashes,' Louise told him fiercely.

'You can come and watch me playing tennis tomorrow if you like,' Oliver was saying to Caesar in an off-hand manner that did nothing to conceal from Louise just how quickly and easily her son could become vulnerable to his father.

Frantically she wondered if it would be possible to change their flights so that they could leave as soon as possible. She could leave her grandparents' ashes here with the priest, surely, and deal with the practical matters of their interment from the safety of London. Caesar couldn't *really* want to be involved in Oliver's life. Even though as yet he didn't have legitimate children, it would only be a matter of time before he married and set out to produce the next Duca di Falconari.

Knowing that should have reassured her, but her heart-rate was refusing to slow down and her body was a mass of jangled nerve-endings. Even when she finally pulled her hand away from beneath Caesar's her body was still tingling and, yes, aching with the sensations his touch had aroused inside it. Sensations of anger and…and *loathing*, Louise tried to reassure herself. Given what he had done, how could it be anything else?

'If Oliver's ready, it's time for our junior photography class,' the pretty young girl who was in charge of the children's activities announced, coming over to them.

Both her statement and her smile were for Caesar, Louise noted grimly. She could also see that her son was reluctant to absent himself from the side of his new friend. He scowled at her when she pushed him gently in the girl's direction, and then shook off the hand she had placed on his arm. She didn't like the anger Oliver was showing towards her, but that didn't mean she was willing to accept Caesar's interference, Louise decided.

But immediately Caesar remonstrated with Oliver,

telling him calmly, 'That is not a good way to behave to your mother.'

Oliver looked both upset and mortified, reacting to Caesar's rebuke and disapproval with far more concern that he ever did to hers.

'You had no right to speak to Oliver like that,' she told Caesar as soon as Oliver and the children's activities girl were out of earshot. 'He is *my* son.'

'And mine,' Caesar told her calmly. 'I have received the DNA results and they show that quite clearly.'

Her heart did a double somersault, sending the blood pounding through her veins. Treacherously, shockingly, in a series of unwanted flashbacks, images of the intimacy they had shared to create Oliver played in front of her eyes. She could even feel the emotions she had felt then—the excitement, the longing, the need to be wanted that had been so intense it had driven her to delude herself that she was wanted, that she mattered.

Pain as cruelly stabbing and merciless as it had been then gripped her again. In many ways she might have been the cause of her own misfortune, but Caesar could have treated her more gently. But he was Oliver's father, and there was enough of her grandparents' Sicilian teaching and upbringing in her for her to be unable to deny that that mattered—much as she wished she could.

Even so… 'There is no need for you to tell me the identity of my son's father,' she informed him grimly.

She was like a small soft-boned cat, spitting and hissing her anger as a defence measure, Caesar recognised inwardly. And, like that cat, would she also purr warmly with delight when she was stroked and pleasured?

The way in which his body reacted to that question was like a shockwave of tidal proportions, re-awakening emotions and needs he had thought long suppressed by his self-control.

'We have a great deal to talk about, and I would suggest that the best and most private place for us to do that would be the *castello*.'

'Oliver...' Louise began but Caesar shook his head.

'I have already spoken with the children's activities manager. Oliver will be taken care of until you return.'

The *castello*. The scene of Oliver's conception. Although it was hardly likely that on this occasion she would be visiting Caesar's bedroom. Not that she wanted to do that, of course. Not after the price she had paid for being there before.

'I don't...' she began, but somehow or other Caesar had taken possession of her arm and was guiding her towards the foyer of the hotel and then through it, to where a long black limousine complete with driver was waiting for them.

It was only a twenty-minute drive from the hotel to the *castello*. Caesar probably had a financial interest in the hotel, Louise reflected, since it must have been built on land that belonged to him.

As the car swept through the magnificent gardens to the front of the *castello* Louise tried not to be impressed, but that was almost impossible.

The Falconari family had been on the island for many, many generations. They had married well and accumulated great wealth and it showed. The emblem from their crest, the falcon itself, was emblazoned above the main entrance to the *castello* and incorporated everywhere in the intricate carvings ornamenting the building. The family's stamp on their property. Just as Oliver's looks were his father's stamp upon him.

Louise gave a small shiver. There had been something about the way Caesar had held Oliver earlier, about the way her son had looked up at him, that had hurt her inside—in that place her own childhood had left raw and unhealed. Instinctively, but without wanting to admit it, Louise knew that no child of Caesar's would be denied proper paternal concern. That was the Sicilian way, and the Duca di Falconari Caesar was not just honour-bound but had been raised from birth to respect and follow that code. And what did that mean?

Louise did not want to think about what it meant. Oliver was hers. She had borne him and brought him up alone, and she was fiercely protective of him. She had given herself to his father with all the innocence of her longing to be wanted and valued. Now, in a different way, she had seen in their son's eyes his readiness to turn to his father. She was not going to allow Caesar to hurt and reject their son the way he had done her.

The car came to a halt alongside an imposing flight of marble steps.

No one could fault Caesar's manners, Louise acknowledged as he came round to open the car door for her before escorting her up the steps. But it took more than the outer vestments of showy good manners to make a man a worthwhile human being—the kind of human being who was going to be a good father. Her heart jumped inside her chest wall. Why was she thinking that? Caesar was *not* going to be Oliver's father. And yet Louise knew that it was going to be hard for her to forget the way Oliver had turned to Caesar and not her just before they had left him, moving closer to Caesar and looking almost pleadingly at him.

The main hallway of the *castello* was formidably impressive. Niches in the walls contained pieces of statuary, an airy flight of stairs curled upwards, and the smell from the floral display on an antique table in the middle of the marble-floored room filled its still silence.

'This way,' Caesar told her, indicating a double doorway that opened off the hallway into what Louise remembered from her original visit to the *castello* to be a series of rooms that opened one into the other, each of them decorated and furnished in style, with contents that Louise suspected must be worth several kings' ransoms.

Leading the way through one of them, Caesar pushed open another set of doors onto a covered walkway beyond which lay an enclosed courtyard garden, with a fountain playing and doves cooing from a small dovecote.

'This was my mother's garden,' he told Louise as he gestured to her to sit down on one of the chairs drawn up at a pretty wrought-iron table.

'She died when you were very young I remember my grandmother saying,' Louise felt obliged to offer.

'Yes. I was six. My parents died together in a sailing accident.'

Out of nowhere, without his seeming to do anything to summon her, a maid silently appeared.

'What would you like? English tea, perhaps?'

'Coffee—espresso,' Louise told him, thinking inwardly that she needed the boost an espresso would give her to stand up to Caesar. 'My grandparents taught me to drink it a long time before I developed any taste for English tea. They used to say that it was a taste of home, even though the smell could never be the smell of home.' She wasn't going to admit to him that right now she needed its strengthening qualities.

The maid had gone and come back again with their coffee, only to leave them alone again, before Caesar demanded, 'Why did you not contact me to tell me that you were carrying my child?'

'Do you really need to ask me that? You wouldn't have believed me. Not after the hatchet job the headman had done on my reputation and my morals. No one else did—not even my grandparents at first. It was only when Oliver was growing up that my grandfather asked me if he could be yours. He recognised that Oliver looked like you.'

'But you knew right from the start?'

'Yes.'

'How? How could you know?'

A tiny wire of pain drilled through her, but her pride refused to allow her to dwell on it, commanding her instead to suppress it.

'That's none of your business. Just as Oliver himself is none of your business.'

'He's my son, and in my book that makes him very much my business—as I have already told you.'

'And I have already told you that I am not going to allow you to force my child to grow up as your illegitimate son—even though here in Sicily that is perfectly acceptable for a powerful man like you. I will *not* have my son forced to grow up as someone who is second best—an outsider to your life, forced onto the sidelines to look on and witness your legitimate and more favoured children…' Abruptly Louise stopped speaking, knowing that she was allowing her emotions to betray her, and took a deep breath before continuing more calmly. 'I've experienced first-hand the damage that can be caused to a child by its longing for a parent who cannot or will not engage emotionally. I will not allow that to happen to Oliver. Your legitimate children—'

'Oliver is and will be my only child.'

The quiet words seemed to reverberate around the courtyard before giving way to a shocking silence that Louise was initially unable to find the words to break.

His only child?

'You can't say that. He might be your only child now, but—'

'There will be no other children. That is why it is my intention to recognise and legitimise Oliver as my son and my heir. Oliver will be my only child. There can be no others.'

Louise looked at him, wishing that he wasn't sitting in the shadows and she could see his expression better. His voice was giving him away, though, telling her quite clearly how hard he had found it to make such an admission. It wasn't just his pride that would have made it hard either. Any man would feel a blow to his maleness at making such an admission.

And was she weakening towards him because of that? Did she feel sympathy for him? How *could* she? She could because she was human and she knew what it was to suffer, Louise told herself. That was all. She would have experienced that same sharp pang of disbelief followed by sympathy for anyone making such an admission in a way that told her how hard it was for them to do so. It did not mean… It did not mean what? That Caesar still meant something to her?

His admission, she realised, had her own heart slamming into her ribs and her lungs tightening with disbelief.

'You can't know that,' she protested.

'I can and do know it.' Caesar paused, and then told her in carefully spaced, unemotional words, 'Six years ago, when I was involved in an aid project abroad that my charitable foundation was helping to finance, I was on site when there was an outbreak of mumps. Unfortunately until it was too late I didn't realise that I'd fallen victim to it. The medical results were incontrovertible. The mumps had rendered it impossible for me to father a child. As there is no other male of our blood to inherit the title that meant I had to reconcile myself to the fact that our line would die out with me.'

There was nothing in his voice to betray what that must have meant to him other than a slight terseness, but Louise didn't need to hear it to understand the emotions he must have felt. Knowing his history, knowing the Sicilian way of life, knowing his arrogance, she could easily imagine what a searing, shocking blow such news must have been to him.

'You could adopt,' she pointed out logically.

'And have countless generations of those with Falconari blood turning in their graves? I think not. Historically Falconari men are more used to fathering children on other men's wives than accepting another man's child as their own.'

'Droit du seigneur, I suppose you mean?' Louise challenged him cynically.

'Not necessarily. My ancestors did not have a reputation for needing to force women into their beds. Far from it.'

There it was again, that arrogance and disdain, and yet against her will Louise was forced to acknowledge that it would be unbearably painful for a man with Caesar's family history to accept that he could not father a child— especially a male child.

As though he had read her mind he told her, 'Can you imagine how it felt for me to have to accept that I would be the first Falconari in a thousand years not to produce a son and heir? And, if you can imagine that, then I ask you to imagine how I felt when your grandfather's letter arrived.'

'You didn't want to believe him?'

He gave her a look that enabled her to see the bleakness in his gaze.

'On the contrary. I wanted to believe him very much indeed.'

So much so that the reins to his self-control had slipped from his grasp, and if Louise hadn't come out to Sicily herself Caesar knew he would have gone to seek her out, even though he had warned himself that doing so could expose him to ridicule and rejection.

'I just didn't dare allow myself to believe him, in case he was wrong, but the DNA tests are completely conclusive—even if Oliver had not so physically obviously been a Falconari.'

'My grandparents always said that he looked very like your father as a boy,' Louise admitted reluctantly. 'They remembered him from when they lived in the village.'

'Now no doubt you will understand why I wish Oliver to grow up as my acknowledged son and heir, and I hope that has put your mind at rest with regard to the supremacy of his position in my life as my acknowledged son. Oliver will never need to fear that he will be supplanted by another child. And as I know what it is to grow up without parents you may also be sure that the fathering he receives from me will be true fathering. He will grow up here at the *castello* and—'

'Here?' She shook her head vehemently. 'Oliver's place is with me.'

'Are you sure that is what Oliver himself wants?'

She had been right to be wary of him.

'Of course I am. I am his mother.'

'And I am his father—as the DNA test confirms. I have a father's rights to my child.'

Caesar could feel her rising panic in the air surrounding her. She was like a lioness fighting to protect her cub, he acknowledged with reluctant admiration. She might be having problems with Oliver now, as he grew towards manhood and needed a man's guiding hand, but Caesar

knew from the enquiries he had been making about both
Louise and Oliver that she was a very good mother. To
have grown from the girl he remembered to the woman
she was now must have demanded great strength of character and determination. A child sometimes needed a
mother who understood what it meant to be vulnerable.
Right now, though, he needed to banish any thought of
sympathy he might have towards her. Oliver was his son,
and he was determined that he would grow up here on
Sicily.

'I won't have him spending part of his time here and
part in London. It wouldn't be fair on him. He'd be torn
between the two of us and two separate lives,' Louise
announced.

Silence.

She tried again.

'I will not have Oliver sacrificed to some…some ancient role you want him to play. He's a boy. He knows
nothing of dukedoms and the history of the Falconaris.'

'Then it's time for him to begin to learn.'

'It's too much of a burden to put on him. I don't want
him growing up like you.'

The gauntlet had been thrown down now, and it lay
between them in the swirling silence.

Why wasn't Caesar objecting to her comment? Why
wasn't he saying something? Why was she feeling so panicked and anxious? Why did she feel that somehow she
had walked into a carefully baited trap and that the walls
of the courtyard garden were actually closing in on her?

'Then you will no doubt agree that the best way for
you to ensure that Oliver grows up with equal input from
both his parents, and that he knows your views, is for you
to be here with him.'

The statement was delivered smoothly, but that smooth-

ness couldn't conceal the formidable determination
Louise could sense emanating from Caesar.

'That's impossible. I have a career in London.'

'You also have a son who, according to your own
grandfather, needs his father. I would have thought that
he is more important to you than your career.'

'You're a fine one to say that when the only reason
you want him is because he is your heir.'

Caesar shook his head.

'Initially when your grandfather wrote to me, yes, that
might have been true, but from the minute I saw him,
even before I had the results of the DNA test, unbeliev-
able as it may sound to you, I loved him. Don't ask me
to explain. I can't.' He had to turn away from her a little
because he felt so vulnerable, but he knew that he had to
be honest with her if he wanted his plan to succeed. 'All I
can tell you is that in that moment I felt such love, such a
need to protect and guide him, that it was all I could do to
stop myself from gathering him up to me there and then.'

His words evoked some of what she had felt after giving birth to Ollie, after looking at the child she hadn't
wanted, a boy so like his father—she had known immediately the surge of fiercely protective love that Caesar
had just described.

'Of course Oliver is more important to me than my
work,' she answered truthfully.

'There is no greater gift a parent can give a child than
the security of growing up in a family unit that includes
both parents,' Caesar told her, without commenting on
her response. 'For Oliver's sake it seems to me that the
very best thing we can do for our son is to provide him
with the stability that comes from knowing that his parents are united, and here on Sicily, in my position, that
means married.'

CHAPTER FIVE

'Married!'

Just speaking the word left her throat feeling as raw as her shocked emotions were beginning to feel.

'It's the best solution—not just to the situation with Oliver but also to the situation with your grandparents and the effect the past has had on their family reputation.'

'The shame I brought on them, you mean?' Louise demanded angrily, as she tried to focus on what Caesar was saying and fight down the panic that was threatening to seize her. How could she marry Caesar? She couldn't. It was impossible, unthinkable.

But not, apparently, as far as Caesar was concerned, because he was continuing, 'At the moment the village remembers you as a young woman who shamed her family with her behaviour. That shame is, according to our traditions, carried not just by you but also by your family—and that means your grandparents and Oliver. If I were simply to legitimise Oliver and make him my heir that would remove the shame from him, but it would not remove it from you or from your grandparents, and that in turn would be bound to affect Oliver. There would always be those who would seek to remind him of your shame, and in the future that could impact on his ability to be a strong *duca* to his people. If, on the other hand, I marry you and thus legitimise our relationship that would immediately wipe out all shame.'

So many different emotions were struggling for supremacy within her that Louise simply could not voice any of them. More than anything else she longed to be in a position to throw Caesar's arrogant and unwanted offer back at him—just as she longed to tell him that in her opinion the people who ought to be ashamed were him, for publicly shaming her, and those who had welcomed that shaming for the opportunity it had given them to judge a naive eighteen-year-old. However she knew there was little point—not when even her own grandparents had subscribed to the values of their community and stoically borne the stigma of that shame without complaint.

'As my wife you would be raised above the past. So would your grandparents, and so, of course, would Oliver,' Caesar continued.

He could imagine the thoughts that would be going through her head—the battle between her love for her son and her own personal pride. Caesar frowned. It kept catching him off guard that he should feel so attuned to her, but he couldn't deny that he did. Was it because she had borne his son, or because of Louise herself? He could feel the grim ache of an old self-inflicted wound and its shameful scar. He might not be prepared to admit it to her—after all he could barely admit it to himself—but despite that he knew he would never escape from the burden of his own responsibility for the humiliation she and her family had suffered.

He had allowed her to be punished because the ease with which his desire for her had overwhelmed his self-control had been an almost unbearable blow to his pride. He hoped he had learned since then to recognise that strength came from acknowledging one's vulnerabilities, not in trying to deny them.

He had no idea what had caused that lightning spark of furious, fierce connection he had felt with her, that indrawn breath taken out of time when something deep and meaningful passed between them. He had wanted her and he had been ashamed of that wanting, so he had denied both it and her. He could have stayed at the *castello*. He could have delayed the business meetings he had had in Rome. But he hadn't. Instead he had walked away from her, and in doing so had destroyed something very special.

Louise would never know how often over the years he had thought about her and his guilt. He would certainly not burden her with any of that now, knowing that the fact she had never replied to his letter begging her for forgiveness told him exactly what she felt about him and his betrayal.

Marriage to him now would restore her honour, and that of her family, but it would not free him from the burden of guilt he would always have to carry. That she wanted to refuse him was obvious to him, but he could not allow her to do so. Oliver was his son, and he must grow up here into his rightful inheritance. He was, he recognized, asking her to make a very big sacrifice, and the only comfort he could find in doing so was to tell himself that since there was no one in her life, nor had there been for many years, she was not looking for a relationship in which she could give her love to the man who partnered her.

'You have told me more than once how important both Oliver and your grandparents are to you,' he reminded her. 'Now you have the opportunity to prove that by agreeing to my proposition.'

He had her tricked and trapped, Louise recognised. If she refused then he would accuse her of putting her own interests before Oliver and her grandparents. She wasn't eighteen and vulnerable any more, though. He didn't hold all the cards. Oliver was her son. Once she returned to the hotel she could book them onto the first flight on which she could find seats, and once they were back in London they could come to some arrangement over Oliver that was on her terms, not Caesar's.

It seemed, though, that he had guessed what she was thinking, because he announced grimly, 'If you are thinking of doing something rash, such as leaving the country and taking Oliver with you, I would advise against it. There is no way my son will be able to leave the island without my permission.'

Louise could feel her heart filling with sick misery as the reality of the situation sent it plunging downwards as though it was weighted with a stone. Caesar had the power to enforce his threat, Louise knew. However, she still had one card left to play.

'You have talked a lot about me putting Oliver first, but perhaps you should be asking yourself if you should do the same. You want to claim Oliver as your son. You want him to live here and be brought up as your son and heir, but it doesn't seem to have occurred to you how shocked Oliver is going to be to learn that you are his father. It isn't something that can just be announced to him out of the blue. It will take time to prepare him for that kind of information. Even when he does know, and even if he is prepared to accept that you are his biological father, he might choose to reject you.'

'Encouraged to do so by you, you mean? That would be a very Sicilian form of revenge, I agree.'

'I would never do that.' Louise's shocked anger showed

in her voice. 'I would never use my son's emotional happiness to score points over you. He means far too much to me for that.'

'If you really mean that then you will allow him to know the truth without any delay. Oliver is desperate to know about his parentage. I was able to work that out for myself just by his manner towards me, even without the contents of your grandfather's letter. It is my belief that he will welcome the news that I am his father.'

Louise sucked in her breath, her gaze brilliant with angry contempt at his arrogance.

'I also believe that the sooner he is told the better—especially if at the same time we tell him that we are going to be married, and that in future both he and you will be living here with me,' Caesar continued.

'And *I* believe that you are rushing things, and you are doing that for your own sake, not Oliver's. It's all very well for you to talk about rescuing my reputation and therefore that of my grandparents by marrying me, but the reality is that what you are doing is blackmailing me into marriage.'

'No. What I am doing is trying to point out to you the benefits for Oliver of a marriage between us. What I am doing is putting the interests of our son first and suggesting that you do the same.'

'But there's no…no love between us. Marriage should be based on shared love.' It was all Louise could think of to say.

'That's not true,' Caesar contradicted her immediately.

For a moment her heart leapt, and she wanted to cry out against what that meant. She *couldn't* want Caesar to claim that he loved her, could she?

'We both love our son,' he continued, thankfully oblivious to her own reaction to his words. 'We owe it to him to give him the loving, stable childhood that comes with having both his parents there for him and united in their love for him. We both missed out on that, Louise. Me because I was orphaned and you because…' He had to turn away from her, so that he didn't betray how shocked he had been when his enquiries had revealed to him how emotionally barren her own childhood had been.

'Because my father didn't want me?' Louise supplied sharply for him.

'Because neither of your parents put you first,' Caesar told her. 'I know this isn't easy for you, Louise,' he continued. 'But you aren't the only one who feels that mutual love and respect is the best basis for an adult relationship as close as marriage. I share that belief.'

There it was again. Her heart was thudding—slamming, in fact, into her chest wall. As though she was still that vulnerable eighteen-year-old, helplessly in love with Caesar.

'But of course we both know that such a relationship isn't possible between *us*.'

Of course they did. Caesar had never loved her and could never love her. Did she want him to? No…no, of course not.

'I do know how you feel about me,' Caesar continued, causing her to go hot and cold all over. Did he actually dare to think she still cared about him? 'How could I not when you never replied to my letter.'

Now he had thrown and confused her.

'What letter?' she asked him.

Caesar hesitated. He had allowed himself to drop his guard too much already, but now that he had gone this far he knew that Louise would insist on an explanation—as she had every right to do.

'The letter I sent you when I got back from Rome, apologising for my behaviour and asking you to forgive me.'

He had written to her? He had asked for her forgiveness? He had apologised? Her mouth had gone dry. It was inconceivable that he was lying. She knew that instinctively, just as she knew what it must have cost him all those years ago to make such a gesture and now to admit to it.

'There was no letter,' she told him, her voice low and husky. 'At least I never received one.'

'I sent it your father's address.'

They looked at one another.

'I…I expect he thought he was protecting me.'

Caesar's heart ached for her. If she needed him to pretend he believed that then he would do so.

'Yes, I expect so,' he agreed.

He had written to her and her father had kept his letter from her. Please don't let that acid-hot burn behind her eyes be tears. That would be too shaming. It had only been a letter of apology, she reminded herself, nothing more. Exactly the kind of thing a young man of Caesar's upbringing and position would expect of himself: a neat tying-up of unwanted loose ends so that he could draw a line under what had happened between them.

Caesar's crisp, 'It's the present we're living in now, Louise, not the past,' only confirmed what she had been thinking, and he continued equally crisply, 'We both have a duty to the child we created together that I believe goes much further than any of our own needs. I appreciate that a loveless marriage is the last thing you want, but I can promise you that for Oliver's sake I am prepared to do whatever it takes to be in his eyes a good husband as well as a loving father.'

A loveless marriage. How those words appalled her. But she couldn't ignore or deny Caesar's claim that they both needed to put Ollie first. It was ironic that he should be the one to throw that challenge at her when putting her son first had been what she had done from the moment of his birth, for all those years in which Caesar had neither known nor cared about his existence. She didn't doubt Caesar's love for their son, but it was also true that he had an ulterior motive for wanting him in his life. As he had said himself, Oliver was his rightful heir.

Heir to a feudal system and customs that she herself loathed. However, Oliver wasn't her. Louise didn't want to think about how he might feel if somehow she managed to keep him away from Caesar and he didn't learn about his heritage until he was adult. There was a lot of Falconari in Oliver. She knew that. And did she want it fostered so that he could become as arrogant and as steeped in privilege as his father?

No. All she wanted was for him to be happy and fulfilled. And if she married Caesar and stayed here wouldn't she have far more opportunity to guard and guide her son so that whilst he grew up aware of his heritage she could see to it that he also grew up aware of how much its feudal systems needed to be changed?

She was weakening, giving in…

'You speak of being a good husband, but everyone knows that Falconari wives are expected to remain in the background, being dutiful and biddable. I can't live like that, Caesar. Apart from anything else I want Ollie to grow up respecting my sex and its right to equality.'

She paused to take a deep breath, but before she could continue Caesar took the wind out to of her sails completely by responding, 'I totally agree.'

'You…you do? But there's my career…' The career

she'd worked so very hard for. 'You can hardly think that
I'd give up doing the work I've trained and qualified for,
which I know benefits others, to be...'

'Oliver's mother?'

'To be the Duchess of Falconari,' Louise corrected
him.

'No. I can't and I don't. It is my hope that within my
lifetime I can help my people to step forward into the
twenty-first century. You, with your expertise and training, could help me in that work, Louise. You could have
a very important role to play in helping me to change the
old order and equip my people for the modern world if
you chose to stand at my side and do so.'

Change the old order? Oh, yes. Only now that Caesar
had spoken the words did she know how very much she
wanted to be part of that.

'Just as we can raise our son together, so we can lead
our people together—the people who will one day be his
people. I may have no right to ask for it, Louise, but I
need your help to change things for Oliver's sake—just as
you need mine to make sure that our son grows up knowing what it is to have a father who loves him as well as a
mother, two parents who are united in their love for him.
All you have to do is say yes.'

'Just like that? That's not possible.'

'Oliver's conception shouldn't have been possible, and
yet it happened.'

She was weakening again, and she knew it. Caesar cast
a powerful spell around her that robbed her of the ability
to think straight. When she was with him... When she
was with him she wanted to go on being with him. But
in a loveless marriage?

Caesar might not love her, but he did love Ollie. She
couldn't deny that. He had been sincere when he had spo-

ken of his instant fatherly love for their son—a boy who desperately needed his father.

The point Caesar had made about her reputation and her shame, especially with regard to her grandparents, had touched a nerve. Didn't she owe it to her grandparents as well as to Oliver to do what Caesar wanted?

She had always known that at some stage Oliver would have to know not just the identity of his father but the circumstances surrounding his conception. That had always worried her. Which was why she had been so reluctant to tell him what had happened until she had felt he was old enough to be able to deal with that kind of information.

Even so, she wasn't going to give in without a fight.

'It's all very well you claiming that my shame will be wiped out by marriage to you, but there is bound to be gossip about the past. I've always protected Oliver from… from what happened. Once he's acknowledged as your son, even if you legitimise him and marry me, people are bound to talk. Oliver could be hurt by what he might hear. I can't allow that.'

'You won't have to allow it. Naturally when I announce that Oliver is my son and that you and I are to marry I shall discreetly let it be known that my own behaviour during that summer was not as it should have been, and that my feelings for you and my jealousy because of the interest being shown in you by other young men led me to fail in my duty to protect you. I shall say that when I asked you to marry me then you refused. You were a modern girl, a young modern girl, who had her own plans for her future. I had to let you go. On your return visit here we both discovered that those old feelings were still very strong, and this time when I proposed you accepted.'

'You would do that?'

It was a generous offer, and it caught her off guard,

undermining her defences. Something inside her couldn't help wondering what it would be like to have the protection of a man like Caesar who genuinely loved you. She mustn't even *think* about asking herself that question, Louise warned herself. It made her far too vulnerable.

'Yes, of course. If you were my wife it would be my duty to protect your reputation.'

Ah, of course. It wasn't *her* he would be protecting, *her* to whom he would be making amends for old wounds inflicted, it would be her position as his wife.

'If your grandfather was alive he would want you to accept my proposal for both your own and Oliver's sake.'

'How much emotional pressure are you intending to put on me?' Louise challenged him.

'As much as it takes,' he responded, unabashed. 'There are two ways we can do this, Louise. The first is calmly and matter of factly—with both of us working together in Oliver's best interests to provide him with the most secure emotional life we can, with both of us here for him as his parents within marriage. The other is for us to battle it out for him and for his loyalty and risk, as we do so, inflicting the most terrible emotional damage on him.'

'You've forgotten the third alternative.'

'And that is?'

'That you forget that Oliver is your son and you allow him and me to return to our lives in London.'

The words *the way you did me* hung in the air between them, unspoken, but Caesar proved to her that he knew what she was thinking when he said curtly, 'I can never forgive myself for being weak enough to allow Aldo Barado to persuade me of the damage it would do to both of us if it got out that you had spent the night with me. He had seen you leaving the *castello*, you see, and he said...'

'That you must not allow yourself to be associated with

me—a girl he himself had denounced as a little tart set on seducing the village boys.'

'It was the act of a weakling—a man who could not face up to his responsibilities, a man who allowed someone else to make his decisions for him.' And it had also been the act of a man panicked into fleeing as fast as he could from the surging strength and power of an emotion he hadn't been able to control. But he couldn't tell her that. After all it had taken him long enough to admit it to himself—all those nights in his early twenties spent lying awake in bed next to a woman he had just possessed only to find himself filled with distaste for what he had done, conscious of an emptiness within him that had become such a permanent ache it had become ground into him.

From somewhere deep inside her Louise was conscious of her professional voice telling her quietly, *It was the act of an orphaned twenty-two-year-old, carrying a heavy weight of huge responsibility and deliberately manipulated by a powerful older man who had his own agenda to protect.*

Was she making allowances for him? Wasn't that what her training had taught her to do? To look behind the façade and dig deep into what lay behind it?

'I can't let you deny our son his heritage, Louise. He has a right to grow up knowing what it is—good and bad—just as he has a right to reject it when he has grown up if that is his wish.'

He was sounding so reasonable that it was hard for her to throw emotional arguments at him. They would sound selfish—as though she wasn't thinking of Oliver, as though she wasn't listening to him.

'I know how much I'm asking of you in Oliver's name, but I also know that you are strong enough to accept the challenges that lie ahead.'

Oh, how underhand—to praise her like that and so undermine her.

'If I let you walk away would it genuinely be the right thing for Oliver?' Caesar shook his head. 'I don't think so. How is he going to feel about himself and about you, do you think, if you deny him the right to know his real heritage and to know me with it until he is old enough to discover it for himself? Are you really willing to risk inflicting that kind of damage on him just to keep him away from me?'

Of course she wasn't. How could she? If she was honest with herself, the thought of a loveless, sexless marriage—with anyone other than Caesar—didn't bother her. After all, she had already decided a long time ago, in the aftermath of the fall-out from Oliver's conception, that given her apparent drive to pursue men who would only withhold their love from her it was far better for her not to get emotionally involved. After all, what patterns might he learn about man-to-woman relationships if he had to witness his own mother denigrating herself, constantly seeking the love she was being denied?

If she acceded to Caesar's proposition she would be in a position where she would have some power within their relationship from its start, and be in a position to set boundaries for Oliver's emotional security in all aspects of his growing up.

And finally she knew that this outcome, a marriage between her and Caesar so that Oliver could grow up with both his parents and legitimacy, would have delighted both her grandparents. They had made so many sacrifices for her—not just in taking her in when she had been so disgraced, but in helping her to learn to be a good mother, in supporting her when she had decided to return to her education, and in giving both her and Oliver the most wonderful and loving home.

She took a deep breath and stood up, walking several yards away from Caesar and into a patch of sunlight in a deliberate move intended to bring him out of the shadows so that she could see his expression when she spoke to him.

'If I were to agree to your proposition there would be certain terms, certain boundaries with regard to your attitude towards me and how that could impact on Oliver, that I would want guaranteed. However, more important than that, indeed of first importance, is Oliver himself. It is true that he is angry with me because I have refused to discuss the identity of his father with him, and it is true, I agree, that he is missing his great-grandfather's male influence in his life. As I myself know, however, a bad father can be more damaging than an absent one.

'You have your own reasons for wanting Ollie, and in spite of what you say you aren't in a position to claim that you love him as your son. You don't know him. He doesn't know you. I am concerned that in the first flush of excitement in discovering that you are his father Ollie might be swept into a son-and-father relationship with you before he really knows you, and that he will have expectations of that relationship that are too idealistic and cannot be met. For that reason I think it is better that Ollie gets to know you better before we tell him about the relationship you share.'

As she had hoped he would, Caesar stepped out of the shadows and came towards her. But any comfort she might have derived from being able to see his expression was more than offset by the rejection of what she had said that she could see so plainly in the hardening of the fiercely strong bone structure of his face.

Even his eyes, the same unexpected and steely grey as Oliver's, were darkening as he looked directly at her before saying arrogantly, 'I don't agree. Oliver is obviously an intelligent boy. We look far too alike for him not to put two and two together. Any delay in confirming our relationship could lead to his feeling that I am assessing him, perhaps delaying claiming as my son because I do not entirely want him.'

Thinking of her son's defensive and prideful nature, Louise gave a reluctant nod.

'I see your point. But what will we tell him about our past?'

He had an answer for that too—as he seemed to for everything.

'That you and I parted after a quarrel, during which you told me never to contact you again, before returning to London in the belief that I would not want to know about my child.'

Louise wanted to object to the half-truth, but the practical side of her recognised that for a boy of Ollie's age such a simple explanation would be far easier for him to deal with and accept than something more emotionally complex.

'Very well,' she agreed grudgingly, 'but before anything is said to Oliver he needs to have the opportunity to get to know you.'

'I am his father,' Caesar told her, 'and because of that he knows me already via his genes and his blood. The sooner he is told the better.'

'You can't just expect me to tell Oliver that he is your son and for him to welcome that.'

'Why not?' Caesar demanded with a dismissive shrug. 'If the way Oliver has already responded to me is anything to go by, he wants a father desperately. Can't you accept that maybe there is something that goes beyond logic, and that he and I instinctively sense we have a blood tie?'

'You are *so* arrogant,' Louise protested. 'Oliver is nine years old. He doesn't know you. Yes, he wants a father, but you must be able to see that because of his situation he has created an idealised version of the father he wants.'

'And whose fault is that? Who refused to allow him to understand and accept the real situation?'

'What I did, I did for his sake. Children can be just as cruel as adults—even more so. Do you really think I wanted him going through what I had to endure myself, and with much less reason? I was to blame for my own situation. I broke the rules. I shamed my family. All Ollie has done is be born.'

She really loved the boy, Caesar recognised as he heard the protective maternal ferocity in Louise's voice. With the pride he could hear ringing in her voice it must have been hard for her to bear the condemnation of society for so long. Whilst *he* had had no payment to make at all. Other than within himself, of course. There he had paid over and over again.

'We shall be married as quickly as it can be arranged. I have a certain amount of influence that should help to speed up the necessary paperwork. It is my belief that the sooner we are married the more speedily Oliver will be able to settle down in his new life here on the island, with both his parents.'

Louise's heart jerked as though someone had it on a string. Although Caesar had said they must marry, somehow she'd been so preoccupied with worrying about how Oliver would react to the news that Caesar was his father that she had put the issue of the actual marriage to one side. Now, though, Caesar's words had put the full complexity of the situation in front of her like a roadblock.

'We can't get married just like that,' she protested. 'I have a job, commitments. My home is in London—Oliver goes to school there. We can tell Oliver that you are his father and that we plan to marry, then Oliver and I can return to London, and in a few months' time—'

'No. Whatever you choose to do, Oliver stays here with me. I can make that happen,' he warned her when she started to shake her head.

Louise could feel her body starting to tremble inwardly. She knew that what he was saying was true, and she knew too how ruthless he could be when it came to protecting his own interests. Oh, yes, she knew that. She wasn't going to give up without a fight, though. Not this time.

'I have responsibilities. I can't just abandon my life to marry you.'

'Why not? People do it all the time. We're two people who engaged in a passionate night together which resulted in the birth of a child,' she heard Caesar continuing bluntly. 'We parted, and now life has brought us together again. In such circumstances no couple would wait months in order to be together. Apart from anything else, I don't think it would be good for Oliver. Knowing that we quarrelled and parted once could lead to him becoming anxious about the same thing happening again.'

'People are bound to talk and gossip.' Louise knew that it was a weak argument, but something deep within her, a vulnerability and a fear she didn't dare allow herself to acknowledge for what it really was, had sent her into panic mode.

She was frightened of being married to Caesar. Why? The foolish, reckless girl who had had no thought of protecting herself from emotional self-harm had gone. She was a woman now. That brief foolish longing to find what she had believed she so desperately needed in Caesar's arms and in Caesar's bed had been analysed and laid to rest a long time ago. She had no vulnerability either to Caesar himself or to the intimacy the institution of marriage was supposed to represent.

'Briefly, yes, but once we are married, and it can be seen that we are just as any other couple with a child to bring up, such talk will soon be forgotten. Once we are married my people will be far too delighted to know that I have an heir to dwell on past scandal.'

He looked at his watch.

'It is time for us to collect Oliver.'

It was the reality of what lay ahead of her that pierced her heart so sharply, Louise assured herself as they left the *castello*, and not that small word *us*.

'And he really is my father?'

It was gone eleven o'clock at night. Oliver was in bed in their hotel room and should have been asleep, but instead he was wide awake and still asking questions almost non-stop after Caesar had made his calm announcement to Oliver that he was his father.

'Yes, he really is,' Louise confirmed for the umpteenth time.

'And now we're going to live here and you are going to get married?'

'Yes, but only if that's what you want.'

Louise still felt it would be far better to give Oliver more time to adjust to the fact that Caesar was his father and to get to know him more before any future commitments were made, but Oliver, it seemed, shared his father's views on the subject of them immediately forming a legal family bond—as he had made very plain to her.

'You and Dad will get married soon and we'll all live together here like a proper family, won't we?' he pressed her.

'Yes,' Louise agreed hollowly, before reminding him, 'It will mean a big change for you, Ollie. You've got your schoolfriends in London, and…'

'I'd rather be here with Dad and you. Besides, they were always asking me why I didn't know who my father was and making jokes about me. I'm glad that I look like him. Billy's dad said so when he saw us together. I look more like him than I do you. Why didn't you tell me before?'

'I was waiting until you were older, Ollie.'

'Because you'd quarrelled and he didn't know about me?'

'Yes.'

Watching him stifle a yawn, Louise could see that the events of the day were catching up with him. Switching off the lamp, she walked out onto the small balcony, closing the door behind her to give Oliver time to fall asleep.

Watching Ollie with Caesar earlier, she'd had to admit against her will how alike they were—not just in looks but somehow in temperament and mannerisms as well. It was as though being with his father had brought to life that proud lordly Sicilian male inheritance that was so much a part of Caesar's personality. No one seeing them together earlier could have doubted that they were father and son. But what had surprised her most of all, when it had been time for them to part, had been the unexpected but totally natural way in which Caesar had hugged his son, and Ollie, who was normally so wary of being touched even by her, had hugged him back.

For a handful of seconds watching them together she had actually felt shut out and excluded. Afraid that Ollie would form such a strong bond with his father that he would resent and blame her if she tried to delay things. Ollie was too young to understand that all she wanted to do was to protect him from any possible future hurt.

But Ollie wasn't the only one Caesar had embraced before he left.

It was a warm balmy evening, and there was no real need for her to give that small shudder as she walked out onto the balcony—unless of course it was because her flesh was remembering the way in which Caesar had turned to her after he had hugged Ollie goodnight, his hands curling round her upper arms, bare beneath the cream wrap she had worn over a plain cream dress. She didn't have many formal clothes. There was no need, given her almost non-existent social life, and the dress was only a simple linen shift—nowhere near as glamorous as some of the outfits she had seen other hotel guests wearing. It was three years old, and she had noticed that it was hanging a little loosely on her, but then that was surely only natural with the upset both she and Ollie had suffered with the death of her grandfather.

What surely wasn't natural, though, was the way in which her own hands had now moved to the place where Caesar's had held her upper arms before he had leaned towards her in the privacy of the corridor after he had escorted them both to their room, the height and muscular leanness of his body blotting out the light. She could feel the self-conscious burn of angry embarrassment heating her skin even though she was alone on the balcony. How stupid it had been of her to close her eyes like that—as though…as though in anticipation of his kiss. What she had really wanted to do was blot out his image, just as given the chance she would like to blot Caesar himself out of their lives completely.

A fresh shudder ripped through her as she relived the sensation of Caesar's warm breath against her face, the unexpected smoothing movement of the pads of his thumbs against the vulnerable flesh of her arms, her awareness in every pore of her physical proximity to him and how once she would have given anything and everything for that proximity. And that was the reason—the only possible reason—why she had felt that telltale unstoppable rush of overpowering female awareness of him as a man rushing through her body. It was a reaction that belonged to her past. It meant nothing now. It certainly could not be allowed to mean anything.

The shudder that gripped her was one of self-revulsion. And fear? No! She had nothing to fear in any kind of reaction she might have to Caesar Falconari. And that ache that had permeated her body so treacherously? A delusion. Nothing more, brought on by her sensitivity to Ollie's obvious and naturally immature longing for his parents to be 'happy' together. For a second, because of their closeness, her body had read her son's wish and translated it—briefly—into physical reality. That meant nothing. She would not allow it to mean anything.

Their marriage was to be a business arrangement, a pact between them that they had made and would keep for Ollie's sake. There was nothing personal in their relationship for her, and nor did she want there to be.

In the library of the *castello* Caesar frowned as he looked down at the papers on his desk. They had been faxed to him earlier in the evening by the team of very discreet investigators he had commissioned to report to him on every aspect of Louise's life—past and present. She was the mother of his child and it was only natural that he should want to know everything there was to know about her—especially in view of what he already did know about her—for the sake of their son.

It had been obvious to him from the minute he had seen her in the churchyard that there had been a profound change in her from the girl she had been to the woman she now was. He had been prepared for the reports to confirm that change. What he had *not* been prepared for had been to see laid bare, in economical words that somehow made the revelation all the more unpalatable and shocking, the reality of what the child Louise had had to endure at the hands of both her parents but specifically those of her father.

The report simply stated facts; it did not make judgements. What it had said, what it had revealed, was that even before her birth Louise had been rejected by the father who had seen her only as an obstacle to his own ambitions. He had in effect blamed Louise for her own conception, and had gone on blaming her and rejecting her throughout the whole of their relationship whilst she had tried desperately to win his love.

To have the reality of what she had suffered laid bare before him in a form that he couldn't ignore or reject filled Caesar with a mix of anger, pity and guilt. Anger against the father who had treated his own child in such a way, pity for that child herself and guilt for his own part in Louise's shaming and humiliation. *Why* had he not taken the time to look more deeply, to question more closely and see what he should have seen instead of closing his eyes to it? Did he really need to ask himself that question? Wasn't the answer that it had been because he had been too wrapped up in his own fury against himself for wanting someone he had considered unworthy of his desire?

She had come to him wanting a connection, the bond

she had been denied by her father, but he had not allowed himself to see that. Instead he had dismissed her, because selfishly he had been afraid of the intensity of his longing for her and the emotions she had aroused in him. He hadn't taken the time to look beneath the surface. Just like everyone else in her life apart from her grandparents he had dismissed her and her feelings as unimportant. Caesar swallowed hard against the bitter taste of his own regret. He prided himself on his care of his people, on taking the time to listen to them and help them with their problems, on having wisdom and compassion and seeing beyond the obvious. He prided himself on extending all of those things to others but he had withheld them from Louise, who had probably had more need of them than anyone else.

Because he had desired her. Because somehow she had touched a place within him that made him burn for her. That had made him feel humiliated, so he had punished her for that and for his own vulnerability.

His behaviour had been unforgivable. Unforgivable and shameful. It was no wonder Louise was so hostile towards him.

But the reality was that between them they had created a child—their child, his son. Oliver whom they both loved. He looked at the report again. What courage and strength it must have taken for a girl hurt and rejected, humiliated and shamed as Louise had been, to deliberately and willingly subject herself to the most intense kind of professional soul-bearing and to come through that experience, to rise from it as she had done. He admired her for that. He admired her and she despised him. But she *would* marry him—for Oliver's sake.

CHAPTER SIX

'I NOW pronounce you man and wife. You may kiss the bride.'

Louise tensed as Caesar leaned towards her to kiss her formally and briefly on the lips. The second kiss to seal their marriage, since they had already gone through the formal service once in Italian before it had been repeated in English.

The ceremony was taking place in the private chapel of the Falconari *castello* itself. The Bishop, a second cousin of Caesar's, had travelled from Rome to marry them, and to Louise's surprise the wedding was being attended by several local dignitaries and by Caesar's older cousin and her family—her husband and their three sons, the youngest of whom was only eighteen months older than Oliver.

Anna Maria and her family had arrived within three days of Caesar's formal announcement of their marriage, and unexpectedly—indeed reluctantly at first—Louise had quickly discovered that she genuinely liked the no-airs-or-graces Anna Maria, who never used her title and whose husband was an untitled businessman. She had even found herself agreeing to Oliver accompanying Anna Maria and her family on the sightseeing trips they had planned during their visit. She'd agreed because she had seen how much Oliver enjoyed their company, however, rather than because, as Anna Maria had suggested, she and Caesar needed time together on their own. Time alone with Caesar was the last thing she wanted.

Louise knew that Anna Maria had been given Caesar's official version of their past relationship, because whilst thankfully Anna Maria hadn't asked her any difficult questions she had made it very plain that she fully accepted and welcomed both Ollie and Louise herself into the family.

It was only now, with the full weight of the formality of what marrying a man in Caesar's position actually meant upon her, that Louise was able to admit just how daunting she might have found the rush of events and the traditional hoops to be jumped through prior to the ceremony if it hadn't been for the fact that Anna Maria had been on hand to answer her questions and support her when she had needed support.

Louise had wanted the ceremony to be little more than a brief legal formality, and at first had balked at Caesar's plans for something grander, but he had insisted that this was necessary—unless she wanted it to look as though he was ashamed of her and thus give rise to gossip that she might have used Oliver to push him into a marriage he didn't really want. That suggestion had incensed her so much that she had angrily reminded Caesar that *he* was the one who was pushing her into marriage, and not the other way around.

Somehow in the ashes of the heat of the argument that had followed she had discovered that Caesar was to have his way after all, and that their marriage would have all the pomp and circumstance that Caesar felt necessary in order to show his pride in his newly discovered son and his wish to honour the woman who had borne that son as he had put it to her. He had even arranged for there to be a public proclamation to that effect, something which had delighted Oliver, who was slotting into life at the *castello* with an ease that sometimes made Louise feel just a little bit shut out from a side of her son's personality that she could see now came entirely from his father.

Caesar was still holding her hand. He had taken possession of it when he had leaned forward to give her the formal ceremonial kiss. Louise could feel herself starting to tremble. A natural reaction to the stress of what was a very demanding day, that was all, she reassured herself. It had nothing to do with the fact that the hand cradling her own belonged to Caesar. *Cradling?* Her hand? Caesar, who had humiliated her so publicly and who only wanted her as his wife because she was the mother of his son?

Watching the small diamonds and pearls that picked out the family arms on the heavy lace veil Louise was wearing tremble slightly as she stood apparently motionless at his side, Caesar frowned. There was nothing in Louise's poised calmness to suggest that she felt apprehensive or vulnerable, nothing in anything she had said or done to suggest that for any reason at all she might need his support, and yet that small tremor made him instinctively want to move closer to her. Because she was now his wife, and it was his duty as her husband to be her protector at all times and in all things. That was part of the code of his family.

His frown deepened as he looked more closely at her whilst the Bishop spoke some final family prayers. Her choice of a very plain, dull wedding gown from the selection that had been sent at his request from Italy's couture houses was both discreet and appropriate. High-necked, cream and not white, long-sleeved, it should perhaps have looked plain on her, but instead it looked regal and elegant. That she should also have chosen to wear the long

intricately embroidered wedding veil, with its mingling
of the arms and emblems of his heritage, stitched for his
mother by the nuns of the convent her family had en-
dowed for generations, had been a decision that initially
he had put down to his cousin's influence. But she had
soon corrected him, telling him that although at first
Louise had been reluctant to wear something so obviously expensive and fragile, she had changed her mind,
saying that she wanted Oliver to be able to look back and
remember that she had worn things that were memories
of both his paternal grandmother and his maternal great-
grandmother, whose pretty little blue enamelled brooch
Oliver had told him his mother was also wearing.

In Caesar's opinion it would have been better if she
had agreed to wear the family tiara he had offered her
to secure the veil, and if she had not insisted on refusing
the expensive engagement ring he had shown her. But he
had been unable to persuade her to change her stance on
that issue, and now, he decided, the reason he was rub-
bing his forefinger over the plain band of gold he had so
recently placed on Louise's hand was because he felt it
was wrong that it should be worn alone.

Her skin felt soft and smooth, her fingers long and
slender, her nails were discreetly varnished with a soft
pink polish. Out of nowhere his memory conjured up an
image from the past of her hands. It wasn't, however,
the image of those same nails painted dark purple that
was causing heat to flood his lower body, along with an
abrupt, powerful coiling of raw male desire. It was too
late now to banish the memory searing his body: the sensation of those slender fingers curling round his erection,
accompanied by the sound of her indrawn gasp of breath.
Her hand had trembled, he remembered, and then so had
her body as she had leaned over him, touching him as

though she had never touched a man before, making him feel that he himself had never been touched so intimately before, as hot dangerous desire had wrenched him away from his self-control.

He tried to stop the unwanted tide of memories but already his body was reacting to them, reminding him—if he needed any reminder—of how hard and fully he had swollen and stiffened to her touch, of how maddened he had been by what had surely been her deliberately provocative, too delicate, almost hesitant touch. She must have known what she was doing to him and how his flesh had craved her. How angry it had made him to be tormented by her like that. How intensely that torment had increased his desire for her. How driven he had been then to take her and possess her, to punish her for her torment of him. His desire for her had been so hot, so reckless, that it had created the life of their child.

Caesar's touch on her flesh was sending sharp prickles of an awareness Louise did not want jolting like lightning from that point of contact. Lightning. She had always been terrified of storms, ever since her father had lost his temper with her when she'd run to him for comfort during one. The power of such storms to destroy, and her own fear of that power, had never left her—no matter how hard she had tried to rationalise to herself that it had been her father's anger and abandonment of her that she really feared and not the forces of nature.

So what was she afraid of now? What made her treacherously use a mental simile that was linked so strongly to her own vulnerability and fear? Nothing, she assured herself. But she still jerked her hand away from Caesar's touch, tucking it down at her side to conceal its betraying tremble. She had trembled that night when Oliver had been conceived—with need, with longing, with the shock of the intensity of her own female arousal. But most of all later, with the humiliation that Caesar had heaped on her. That would never, ever happen again. The past was over.

Louise forced herself to concentrate on the present. The private chapel was filled with the dignitaries Caesar had insisted must be invited to witness their marriage if it was to be accepted as he wanted it to be, and the air was heavy with the scent of incense as a great peal of triumphant choral music rang out from the organ, signalling that it was time for them to walk down the aisle together as man and wife.

The only reason she was still trembling was because it had been such a busy morning that she had skipped a proper breakfast, and had then had a glass of champagne before the ceremony at Anna Maria's insistence, Louise told herself. It had nothing to do with the fact that the lack of width of the aisle meant that she and Caesar had to walk so close together.

Not that her ordeal was over yet. There was still the formal reception to get through, which was being held in the *castello*'s grandly elegant baroque reception rooms, a long corridor's walk away from the chapel in the older part of the building.

'You're a duchess now, Mum.'

Oliver's wide smile as he came up to her was all Louise needed to see to know how her son was reacting to their marriage. These last few days had brought him out of himself so much, and had given him a confidence and a joy in life that lifted her heart every time she looked at him. For that alone any sacrifice she might have to make was more than worth it—even if there were times when she felt a little hurt by the strength of the bond that was developing between father and son. And that was something on which she couldn't fault Caesar. She had been afraid both that he would over-indulge Oliver and also that he might be too formal and distant with him, but to her surprise—and a little to her chagrin—he seemed somehow to know instinctively how to relate to Ollie.

But now, as she watched her son race off to join Anna Maria's boys, Louise acknowledged that she felt very alone. If only she had her grandparents to turn to. Later in the week there was to be a formal ceremony to inter her grandparents' ashes at the church of Santa Maria.

Louise felt her body tense as she realised that the most senior member of her grandparents' village was heading towards her. It was as headman that Aldo Barado had told Caesar he must not see her again. His had been the loudest and harshest of the voices raised against her by the community all those years ago, and Louise could see that he wasn't exactly enjoying the prospect of paying his respects to her as the wife of his *Duca*. He must be in his late sixties now, Louise reflected.

Although he was supposed to be listening to one of his advisers, trying to persuade him that he had already spent enough on building new schools for his people, Caesar recognised that his attention was wandering, and that moreover his gaze was constantly drifting in the direction of his new wife.

Why? Because he felt protective of her as her husband? Because he now understood just how much she had suffered growing up and felt guilty that he too—however briefly—had been a part of that judgemental group? Because as the mother of his son she should have his public support? Because he was proud to call her his wife, knowing how strong and brave she had been?

Because of all of those facts, and because deep down inside him there was still an ache of desire for her.

Perhaps all those years ago a part of his psyche had some-how recognised what his logical nature and his upbring-ing had rejected: namely that she was not the person she had been made out to be.

Louise seemed to know instinctively how to relate to others, Caesar acknowledged as he watched her mixing with their guests, always listening to them with inter-est, never hurrying them to finish whatever it was they wanted to say, and when she did move on leaving them with an approving smile on their faces. Such a wife could only be an asset to a man in his position. The gauche eighteen-year-old he remembered, determined to kick against authority and cause controversy, had obviously risen like a phoenix from her past to become a beauti-ful, confident woman.

Now, as he watched Aldo Barado approaching her, Caesar excused himself to his companion and made a de-termined path towards them. It was his responsibility, his inbuilt duty, to protect his wife and his son, and he cer-tainly wasn't going to let her down as her father had done.

Was she actually foolish enough to feel relief because Caesar had suddenly materialised at her side seconds ahead of Aldo? Louise derided herself. If so, she was making a big mistake. Caesar and Aldo had been on the same side all those years ago, and that side hadn't been hers, had it?

Her relief quickly turned to a sharp surge of anxi-ety and agitation when Caesar put his arm around her to draw her close, his unexpected movement taking her completely off guard. Even worse, her instinctive defen-sive attempt to keep her body from actually touching his somehow resulted in the pressure of his arm actually causing her to sway into him, just as though she was a weak and adoring fool who actually *wanted* his embrace.

Wasn't it bad enough that he had blackmailed her into this wholly false pretence of a marriage without him heaping even more deceit on her by looking for all the world as though he adored her and they were the only two people in the room?

She hated herself for not being able to break the eye contact he was inflicting on her, and for allowing him to make her a party to this sideshow of husbandly affection. What was even worse was that, given that she knew he was doing it to deceive onlookers, because his own pride could not bear the thought of anyone knowing that he had been forced to marry her in order to be a proper father to his son, her own senses were somehow falling into the trap of actually responding to the fake look of male longing only restrained for the sake of propriety that Caesar was giving her.

It shocked her to her core to feel tiny darts of female heat leaping from nerve-ending to nerve-ending in tiny but devastatingly effective points of fiery awareness. And what shocked her even more was the sudden knowledge that this wasn't the first time she had felt that sensation. Louise could feel self-protective alarm and denial racing down her spine, but it was too late. She was eighteen again, and standing with her grandparents in the village square, watching whilst Caesar strode around it, talking to his people, her attention for the first time in her life focused wholly on a man who wasn't her father and who was affecting her in a totally unfamiliar way.

It was impossible for her to suppress her small betraying gasp. She had buried that moment as deeply as though it had never happened. She wished desperately that it had *not* happened. But the truth was there in the open now, confronting and shocking her. So she had momentarily felt the young woman's reckless thrill of sensual reaction to a good-looking man? What did that mean except that she was human? Nothing. She had soon learned that Caesar was no romantic hero for a naive girl to put on a pedestal and adore.

'My lovely wife.'

The sound of Caesar's voice dragged her back to the present, her body tensing instinctively and immediately when he reached out and drew her towards him, his arm around her waist. He was simply playing a role. She knew that. If she felt acutely aware of him then it was simply because she didn't like the deception she was being forced to share. Nothing to do with the fact that she was acutely aware of the hard male strength of his arm around her in its parody of protection. She certainly wasn't in the least bit vulnerable to the image Caesar was creating, and nor was she vulnerable to those quivers of sensation springing from the contact between their bodies. Even if that contact between them was making her tremble from head to foot.

Caesar could clearly see Louise's rejection of her body's helpless response to him in her gaze. All those years ago she had trembled just as she was doing now— but back then she had made no attempt to conceal her body's reaction to his simplest movement, as though she had been powerless to control her sensual response to him, openly delighting in it instead, as her eager yearning movements towards him had urged him to take what she was offering. Guilt shadowed his own body's automatic response to this unwanted betrayal of her reaction to him. *Why* did it so affect him to see that, though she was so obviously hostile to that reaction, she was incapable of controlling it? What was the matter with him? He wasn't a naive boy to be driven by a need he couldn't control simply because a woman trembled with sensual awareness of him. He had far more important matters on which he needed to focus. It was Oliver who mattered now. Oliver and his future. Oliver's acceptance by his people and with that Louise's acceptance as well.

'You will have to forgive me, Aldo,' he told the village headman. 'I confess I can hardly bear to let Louise out of my sight now that we have found one another again after so many years apart.' As he said the words Caesar recognised how much truth they held. Because if he let Louise out of his sight she was likely to leave and take Oliver with her.

Caesar's voice was warm and soft, his look for her tender and rueful, his hold on her that of a man who had no intention of letting her go—all very much in keeping with the attitude expected from a newly married man re-united with an old and lost love, Louise recognised, but of course none of it meant anything. And did she want it to? No, of course not. She only had to think of the past and the way in which Caesar had treated her and hurt her to know that.

But if that past didn't stand between them, if she was meeting him now for the first time, with no preconceptions to overshadow them…? *Hah*—that was good, when the only reason she was here was because of a very important conception indeed: that of their son. Without Ollie there would be no reason for Caesar to want her in his life, no reason for him to pretend he cared about her, and certainly no reason for him to marry her.

'I can't say that this isn't a surprise,' Aldo Barado responded, before acknowledging grudgingly, 'Although there is no question that the boy has to be yours.'

'No question at all,' Caesar agreed, the hard note of steel in his voice causing Louise's heart to flip over, as though it really was foolish enough to believe that Caesar genuinely wanted to protect her.

'My duchess has been generous indeed in giving me the chance to make up for my past errors of judgement,' Caesar continued. 'And, given the understanding I have discovered in her nature, I am sure she will be prepared to extend the same generosity to others as well.'

Louise's eyes widened slightly as she listened to this exchange. She was under no illusions where Aldo Barado was concerned. He was the one who had kept the gossip flowing and who had stirred up more trouble for her in their community in London. She didn't need her degree to know that he had not been heading for her because he wanted to apologise for the past—far from it.

'I am a very lucky man,' Caesar went on. 'A man who is proud to say how honoured he is to have such a wife, and to have the gift of a son.'

'A son is indeed a great gift,' Aldo Barado agreed.

'Later this week the ashes of my wife's grandparents will be interred at the church of Santa Maria. It will be fitting and respectful for those from the village where they grew up to attend that event. I shall donate a new stained-glass window to replace the one that was broken by last year's storms in honour of their memory.'

Nothing more was said. Nothing more needed to be said.

Louise knew how the community worked. Caesar had given an instruction and Aldo Barado would carry it out. The people of her grandparents' home village would attend the interment of their ashes, and in doing so grant them the respect her grandfather had always wanted. With just a handful of words Caesar had achieved what she could never have made happen. Such was his power. Once he had used that power against her. Now he was using it for the benefit of her grandparents. Because Oliver was his son. That was what mattered to Caesar. Nothing and no one else. Certainly not her. Well, that was fine by her. She didn't *want* to matter to Caesar. Not one little bit. He certainly didn't matter to her.

She waited until Aldo Barado had gone before rounding on Caesar to hiss indignantly, 'There was no need for you to come over. I am perfectly capable of dealing with the likes of Aldo Barado. He might have terrified me as a girl; he might have bullied and humiliated my poor grandparents. But things are different now. And as for what you said about the service. Do you *really* think I want anyone there who has to be bribed to attend?'

'You might see it that way, but to your grandparents and the more traditional amongst the villagers how many members of their community are there *is* important.'

There was too much truth in what he was saying for her to be able to deny it, but at least she was able to tell him curtly, 'You can let me go now. There's no need to go on with the charade. Aldo's gone.'

'His isn't the only scrutiny to which we will be subject,' Caesar told her, keeping his arm around her waist and leaning towards her as though he was about to whisper some private endearment to her rather than having a far more mundane conversation. 'We both agreed that for Oliver's sake it is important that our marriage is accepted as being the result of an old love-match between us. People will expect to see at least some outward evidence of that love—especially on our wedding day.'

With his free hand he tucked a loose strand of her hair behind her ear, his gaze fixed on her mouth as though he was having to restrain himself from kissing her. How was it possible for her lips to burn and swell as they were doing just because he was looking at them, almost caressing them with that assured, tormenting male gaze that lied when it said so publicly that he couldn't wait to crush their softness beneath the fierce pressure of a passionate kiss.

Her face was burning now, her throat aching, her instinctive betraying, *'Don't,'* a suffocating sound of frantic denial.

'Don't what?' Caesar challenged her.

'Don't look at me like that.'

'And how *am* I looking at you?'

'You know perfectly well what I mean,' Louise said shakily. 'You were looking at me as though...'

'As though I want to take you to bed? Isn't that exactly what we've agreed that we want people to think?'

Was it? She couldn't remember them ever discussing the reality of having him look at her the way he was doing now, but somehow her brain was refusing to work, and any idea of cool logical thought was impossible to formulate in the fierce aching heat within her body and her frantic attempts to smother those flames. What was happening to her? It was ten years since she had last lain in a man's arms—ten years since the one and only time she had experienced the intensity of physical desire allied to what she had naively then thought of as love.

'We're married. Surely that's enough to convince them that we want to be together? After all we aren't going to... That is we won't be...'

For all that little tremor earlier, Louise was showing him what really mattered to her—and the truth was that she didn't want him, Caesar recognised. Logic told him that he should be pleased, because the last thing he wanted was the complication that would come from allowing a sexual relationship to develop between them. So why, instead of being pleased, did he feel a sense of chagrin? Male vanity? He hadn't thought himself so shallow. The focus of their marriage was going to be their son. They both knew that. But her reaction now reminded him of an issue they had not discussed.

'Our marriage might be sexless, but I am sure you will that agree that that is something that only you and I should know.'

'Yes,' Louise was forced to agree, and a small shiver chilled through her. Why should she feel so cold and so… so…alone just because Caesar had stated the obvious? After all, she didn't want to have sex with him, did she? Of *course* she didn't.

'And whilst we are on this subject, when it comes to sexual relationships outside our marriage…for the present, whilst Oliver's emotional security must be our priority, it is my opinion that celibacy must be the order of the day for both of us. Since neither of us is currently involved in a relationship—or has been for some time—'

Louise stopped him. 'You've been checking up on me? Digging into my private life?'

'Naturally I wanted to know what kind of men you might have been introducing into my son's life as potential future stepfathers,' Caesar answered her.

'You really think that I would take risks with Oliver's emotional security? The only reason I have agreed to marry you is because you are Oliver's father and he needs you. No matter what my personal opinion of you, I believe that you will put him first and be a proper father to him. Not like…not like what I experienced with my own father.'

Abruptly Louise turned away from him. She was saying too much, giving away too much, revealing her own vulnerability.

It was a relief to see Oliver coming towards her, accompanied by Caesar's cousin's sons. The boys were getting on very well together. Just to see her son's confidence growing and to know he was happy meant that whatever sacrifices she personally had to make would be worthwhile, she assured herself as she listened to Oliver's enthusiasm for a trip that was being planned to a newly opened water park on another part of the island.

One of the happiest and best moments of the day for her was when Anna Maria's husband toasted them as a newly married couple and Oliver, standing next to Caesar, demanded, pink-faced with delight, 'I really have a proper dad now, don't I?'

Caesar immediately got up from his chair to go and hug his son tightly as he told him emphatically, 'You have a father, Oliver, and I have a son. Nothing can ever take that relationship away from us.'

Those words, and the emotions that so plainly went with them, touched a place in her heart that had long hurt her on Oliver's behalf—a place that was now beginning to be salved. It was still a huge risk, a huge act of faith for her to put her trust in Caesar's promise to love their son, but what other choice did she really have when Ollie so plainly wanted Caesar as his father?

Under cover of the others' smiles, she had turned to Caesar and warned him quietly, 'If you ever, *ever* let Ollie down I shall never forgive you.'

In response Caesar had told her, equally quietly but fiercely, 'If I were ever to let him down I would never forgive myself.'

CHAPTER SEVEN

'OH, CAESAR, I nearly forgot! I think the excitement of your marriage must have been a bit too much for your housekeeper. I overheard Signora Rossi telling the maids to make up your parents' old interconnecting state bedrooms for you and Louise this morning, just before I came down to the chapel for the ceremony.'

Caesar's cousin wrinkled her nose and laughed, whilst Louise froze. The adults of the family were in the 'small' dining room—all fifty feet of it—having a brief post mortem on the undeniable success of the day, before retiring.

'So old-fashioned of her—but then, of course, she was your parents' housekeeper. As though you and Louise would want to have separate rooms! I told her to instruct the maids to move Louise's things to your own suite instead. Apart from anything else your suite is so much more modern and comfortable than those dreadfully old-fashioned state bedrooms your parents occupied. I know that for a fact from when she allocated them to Ricardo and me on our first visit after our marriage.' She stifled a small yawn.

Louise had to take a small sip from the brandy glass she had been nursing, her lips trembling against the glass as she did so. She wasn't really a drinker, but Anna Maria's lightly amused words had sent such a shock of dismay through her that she felt she needed the glowing warmth of the spirit to banish that shock's icy coldness.

'You must both be exhausted. I know I am,' Anna Maria continued, thankfully oblivious to the consternation she had caused.

As much as Louise desperately wanted to look at Caesar, to see how he was receiving his cousin's well-meaning interference in his careful arrangements, she couldn't trust herself to do so.

'The boys dropped off the minute they were in bed, didn't they, Louise?' Anna Maria chattered on.

Numbly, Louise nodded her head.

When they had discussed their marriage Caesar had mentioned the fact that for form's sake their marriage must seem 'normal', but that they could get round the fact that neither of them wanted any sexual intimacy with the other by occupying the interconnecting state bedrooms, each with its own bathroom, dressing room and private sitting room, which until his parents' death had traditionally always been occupied by the *Duca* and his duchess.

The rooms need some refurbishment, Caesar had told her when he had shown her over them, and he intended to leave the choice of redecoration of her own rooms to her. He would return to his own suite whilst those renovations were taking place, and she had agreed with him that the arrangement would give them both the physical separation from one another they wanted whilst preserving the fiction that their marriage, and with it their sexual relationship, was that of a normal married couple.

Now, though, it seemed that thanks to Anna Maria their sleeping arrangements had been changed, and Louise knew that she would have to wait until they were finally alone in Caesar's suite before she could give vent to her feelings about that change.

Once they were in Caesar's personal suite of rooms, though, it wasn't her angry dismay at the changes that had been made that occupied her thoughts so much as the emotions gripping her throat and momentarily silencing her as she looked round the familiar space that was Caesar's exclusive territory.

On their first visit to the *castello* it had been her father's girlfriend Melinda who had prettily but determinedly insisted on seeing Caesar's private suite. Her pouting and teasing him about the probability of his bed being covered in decadent black silk sheets had resulted in him admitting them into his private domain. Louise admitted that then she had found the simplicity of the decor in his study-cum-office and adjoining bedroom rather dull and unexciting, after Melinda's deliberate flirtations and sexy verbal build-up. It had only been later, as she'd matured and learned, taught herself to appreciate real style and elegance, that she had come to realise how very smart and understated the colour scheme actually was.

Here in Caesar's private quarters the wooden panelling was painted a soft blue-grey, with deeper toned beautifully soft modern rugs softening the starkness of the marble floor. Modern leather-covered furniture—heritage pieces for future generations, Louise felt sure—broke up the space of the businesslike and yet comfortable space that was the sitting room for the whole suite. Bookshelves and cupboards filled the space either side of the fireplace, and a very modern computer desk set beneath one of the now shuttered windows.

Through the off-white painted double doors she could see into the bedroom—and see the enormous double bed, its bedding folded down at both sides, ready for shared occupation.

Louise couldn't control her reaction—a physical shudder that ripped through her body.

Once before she had shared that bed with Caesar. Shared it? Wasn't it the truth that she had virtually begged him to take her there?

The sheets—white and very, very expensive—were of the finest quality possible, even if back then she had not known enough about such things to recognise that fact, and it was surely safer to focus on that fact and use it to block out those awful unwanted images that were threatening to crash through the barriers she had erected against them.

On one side of the bed were double doors that led to a modern marble-and-glass bathroom with a free-standing bath, and on the other a pair of double doors that led to a dressing room.

She didn't want to be here. It wasn't good for her. Not now, when she was feeling so vulnerable, so aware of the past and its consequences not so much for her or for Caesar but for their son. It was there in that room, in that bed, that he had been conceived. There in that bed that she had somehow convinced herself that Caesar wanted and loved her, despite the obvious evidence to the contrary; there that she had willingly allowed herself to be swept away by needs, desires and emotions she had been pitifully incapable of understanding, never mind resisting.

Out of the corner of her eye she saw Caesar remove the dinner jacket into which he had changed for their evening meal, throwing it carelessly onto one of the off-white leather sofas. As he did so, the fabric of his dress shirt pulled tautly cross his shoulders. Traitorously, shockingly, dangerously, her stomach muscles clenched and her heart rolled over.

Quickly Louise closed her eyes—and then wished she

hadn't as immediately her memory replayed for her images of Caesar kneeling over her, his torso naked, tanned, and gleaming with the fine sweat of male desire. She had reached out to touch him, her fingers so sensitised by her emotions and her need that the sensation of his flesh beneath them had seared itself into her memory for ever. How could the flesh covering such a very male body, hard-packed with muscles and sinews and strong bones, feel so incredibly soft? Throbbing with the life pumped through it by his heartbeat—a heartbeat to which her own had responded, thudding in counterpart to it like a rhythm picked out by the most skilled master musician, lifting her, carrying her, driving her.

Louise could feel her heart remembering that rhythm right now. At her touch Caesar had thrown back his head, the raw sound of his fight to control the need in him she had so deliberately and desperately been trying to arouse breaking the sexual tension of the silence between them, shattering it for ever, before he had made his first, fierce thrust into her body as she offered it up to him. How she had welcomed that act, that possession, that fulfilment of every fevered imagining she had had since she had first looked at him and felt the hot, reckless surge of her own sensuality. How her body had welcomed it too, glorying in the hot explosion of physical pleasure that had rocketed through her.

It was this room that was having this effect on her and dragging her back to the past. This room. Nothing more.

'Why on earth did Anna Maria have to interfere?'

Louise's anguished words had Caesar looking at her.

'She thought she was acting in our interests,' he told her mildly. 'She believes we love one another and is sure it is what we both want. It is regrettable that she did what she did, but natural enough, since she believes that we are lovers newly reunited and thus very eager to be together.'

Why did those words cut so sharply into her emotions? Why did they hurt so much and conjure up such dangerous and painful thoughts and feelings?

'But,' Caesar continued, 'once she and her husband and the children have returned to Rome we can revert to our original arrangements.'

How could he be so relaxed and unconcerned when her stomach muscles and her nerves were screwed up to the point of actual physical discomfort?

'But they're going to be here for another three weeks!'

'The situation is as unwelcome to me as it is to you,' Caesar began, but Louise was too wrought up by the fear brought on by her reaction to her own private memories to listen.

'*Is* it?' she challenged him wildly.

Immediately Caesar's voice hardened as he demanded, 'You cannot mean to suggest that I asked Anna Maria to say what she did to my housekeeper so that you would be forced to share my bed?'

'No. No, of course not,' Louise was forced to concede. 'I didn't mean that at all,' she admitted shakily, adding honestly, 'No one would ever believe that you would need to trick any woman into going to bed with you.'

'Then what did you mean?'

I said what I did because I'm afraid—because my own memories have made me afraid. She couldn't tell him that, even if it was the truth, but she had to say something.

'I meant that knowing how important you consider it that people believe we are reunited lovers you might feel that the two of us having to share a bedroom could be a good idea.'

'There's a certain amount of logic in that,' Caesar agreed.

Logic! He was thinking of logic whilst her senses were screaming out in panic and fear.

'You assured me that I would have my own room,' Louise reminded him, her panic returning.

'And so you will—ultimately. However, for now I'm afraid that we are going to have to share this room.'

'And the bed? Do you expect me to share that with you as well?' she challenged him, unable to hold back her apprehension.

Caesar frowned. 'No. I shall sleep on one of the sofas.'

'For three weeks?'

'For three weeks. However, when the maids come in to make up the room in the morning, they must believe that we have shared the bed.'

Louise nodded her head. What else could she do?

'It's been a long day for you, and I have some work I must do,' Caesar informed her, walking towards his computer desk.

Surely that feeling invading her as he walked away from her wasn't really one of disappointment? The last thing she wanted him to do was make any kind of attempt to establish physical intimacy between them, even if they were married and it was their wedding night, wasn't it? Of *course* it was.

Louise walked towards the open double doors into the bedroom.

She had almost walked through them when she heard Caesar saying casually, 'You've never told me. How was it that you were so sure I was Oliver's father? That you were able to state categorically to your grandfather that I was?'

She couldn't move, transfixed on the spot as though physically constrained there, was able only to turn and look at Caesar as he looked at her. He neither knew nor cared how cruel and hurtful he was being, but *she* cared—she cared a great deal, Louise recognised.

She knew what he was thinking, and what he was implying. Of course she did. How arrogant he was to stand there, inferring that she had selected him from a number of men who might have fathered Oliver and judging her for it when the reality was…

Out of nowhere a fierce wave of pride and anger swept through her, overwhelming caution and self-protection, and before she could stop herself she heard herself telling him fiercely, 'I knew because it could not have been anyone else but you. I knew that you were Oliver's father because you were the only man who could be.'

'You never had any doubts that Oliver was my child?'

Caesar didn't really understand himself why he was questioning her like this, and he understood even less what was driving him to do so. It was as though… As though what? As though he wanted her to tell him that he was the only man she would have *wanted* to father Oliver? That was an emotional need—an emotional desire—to feel connected with her at the very point, the very heartbeat of time, in which they had created their son. That was folly, and dangerous for him to have.

Louise didn't hear the giveaway note of yearning in his voice, reacting instead to her own memories and everything that she had felt—everything she had suffered through going to bed with him. She had suffered dreadfully, and now he was judging her yet again. Her anger was urging her to defend herself by letting him know just how wrong his judgement of her was, driving her into a recklessly fierce, 'No!' quickly followed by a sharp, 'After all I wasn't on the pill, and you were the first man I'd had sex with.'

It took the space of a few heartbeats for Caesar to assimilate the information Louise had just given him.

'You were a virgin?' He was every bit as terse as her own outburst. Something in her delivery of her statement not only left him aware beyond all doubt that it was the truth, but also pierced him to the heart with guilt.

How could he not have known? Of all the memories he had of that night, any thought or indication that Louise had been a hesitant shrinking virgin was not one of them. She had given herself to him with an intensity of passion, touched him with sensual eagerness, driven him so determinedly over the edge of his own self-control. Those had not been the actions of an unwilling virgin. Not the actions of an unwilling *partner*, maybe, Caesar mentally corrected himself, but that did not mean that he had not been her first lover. He had not registered that. He had been so consumed by the conflict raging inside him that he had been oblivious to everything else. His taking of her had been the act of a selfish, spoilt young man, every bit as bad in its way as his shameful public rejection and denial of her later.

The information—the facts relayed to him via the reports he had commissioned on her—had been starkly brief and irrefutable. From the time she had returned to London, unbeknown to him carrying his child, his agents had not been able to find any single solitary piece of information to suggest that she had had any kind of sexual relationship. Previously he had put that down to the shame inflicted on her and her care and responsibility for a young child, combined with the effort it must have taken her to turn her life around. Now he was forced to see it in another light. Was it because of *him*? Because of what had happened between them had she turned to a life of sexual self-denial?

'You were a virgin?' he repeated. His brain might have accepted that reality but his emotions were in turmoil. 'That's not...' *Not what I thought when we first met*, was what he had planned to say. But, Louise wouldn't let him finish.

'That's not possible?' she finished for him. 'I can assure you that it is. Not that I care whether you believe me or not, but at least it means that I knew exactly who Oliver's father was.'

'But you came across...'

'As a little tart who was willing to give out to any boy who asked? Oh, it's all right. I do know what others thought of me and how they judged me. I wanted to be popular. I wanted to be the centre of attention. I was jealous of Melinda and my father's love for her. I wanted my father's attention. I learned young that the best way to get it was by behaving badly, so I became a bad girl, and bad girls are *not* virgins. It was easy enough to pretend to be what I wasn't, and to keep those boys who thought they could use me at bay whilst making my father so angry that he was forced to keep an eye on me.'

'But you went to bed with *me*.'

Too late Louise saw the danger she had created for herself. She couldn't let him guess how truly stupid she had been, how she had naively convinced herself that she meant something to him.

'Yes. Because of who and what you were.'

Caesar was frowning. Any second now he'd start asking questions she knew she could not trust herself to answer.

'Because I thought if my father believed that you wanted me he'd see me differently—as someone of value. After all, how could he *not* value me when you, the most important man in the area, wanted me? I'd heard enough from other girls, seen enough in films, to know how a sexually experienced girl should behave.'

Caesar had to turn away from her. Why hadn't he realised, recognised...*known* how vulnerable she was? He already knew the answer. It had been because he had wanted her. 'If I hurt you...'

The words, low and raw and so unexpected, pierced her defences as painfully as though her heart had been gripped in a falcon's talons, Louise acknowledged. Such a question, such recognition, were the last things she had expected. It would be easy to protect herself by letting him shoulder the responsibility for not realising her innocence, but she could not and would not do that.

'No, you didn't,' she told him quietly. 'I wanted what happened between us, and I pushed you until you wanted it to happen as well. By that time I'd convinced myself that we were both part of a fairytale in which you loved me every bit as much as I thought—foolishly—that I loved you. If my father couldn't or wouldn't love me, then you could and did. Or so I told myself.'

No, he hadn't hurt her physically. Delight and pleasure beyond counting was what he had given her. And for the first time in her life the belief that she was loved. But she could never tell him that.

'Of course I hadn't reckoned on you rejecting me, or my father's anger, never mind getting pregnant.'

Best to make light of such things. They were all in the past now, and she loved Oliver far too much to regret for one minute that she had had him. Because of him she had turned her whole life around after all.

'I didn't have a clue, really—far from learning to love me, my father disowned me completely when he discovered that I was pregnant. Both he and my mother wanted me to have a termination. I hadn't really thought about my pregnancy as a baby until that point, but when they tried to pressure me I just knew that I couldn't. That's when my grandparents stepped in. They were marvellous…wonderful. More loving and generous than I had any right to expect. I promised myself that I would do everything I could to make it up to them for all the hurt and shame I'd caused them and it was a real turning point for me. That's why…that's why it's so important to me that I keep my promise to them. It's the least I can do.'

'I've put everything in hand for the committal of their ashes this coming Friday. The whole village should be there.'

'Thank you.'

Without thinking what he was doing Caesar took a step towards her.

Louise felt her heart drop inside her chest wall with all the speed of the most dangerous of funfair rides. If Caesar were to reach out for her now—if he were to take hold of her, if he were to *kiss* her… A fierce shudder racked her body, its intensity nowhere near as damaging as the ache that right now was filling her lower body.

The sight of Louise shuddering brought Caesar to an immediate halt. She didn't want him. She was making that perfectly plain.

'It's late,' he told her curtly. 'You've had a long day. I suggest you get some sleep.'

Nodding her head, Louise closed the doors that separated the bedroom from the sitting room. Tonight was the first night of her new life as Caesar's wife, and the first of many, many nights when she would sleep alone despite their marriage.

CHAPTER EIGHT

THE first thing Louise saw when their small black-clad procession entered the churchyard to the church of Santa Maria was the large mass of villagers standing respectfully in the shadows of the brooding yews. Aldo Barado was at their head, along with the priest.

Caesar had been right. Her grandparents would have taken it as a great mark of respect to have so many people turn out for the interment of their ashes. And they would have been even more proud of the fact that it wasn't their granddaughter, in an elegant black dress that had been one of a selection Caesar had had sent for her to choose from, who was at the head of their small family mourning procession but instead Caesar himself, walking sombrely carrying one of the two ornate gilded caskets that held their ashes, whilst Oliver walked at his side, dressed in formal black mourning clothes like his father, carrying the other casket.

Even the way they held themselves and walked was exactly the same. Father and son together. Louise was walking behind them in the tradition of a society in which in some instances women were not even permitted to attend funerals. Behind her were Anna Maria and her husband and children, and the bowed heads of the waiting villagers.

A formal funeral service had already been held for both her grandparents at their London church. Today they were simply committing their ashes to eternal rest. But instead of turning towards the area of the churchyard occupied by the newer plots, to Louise's astonishment Caesar turned instead towards the imposing mass of the Falconari family crypt. Its door was already open and containers of fresh flowers were placed to either side of that opening.

It was Aldo Barado who voiced the astonishment and disbelief that she herself could not as he stepped forward and demanded of Caesar, 'They are to be laid to rest in the Falconari crypt?' Disapproval was obvious in his voice and his manner.

'Naturally,' Caesar responded, the tilt of his head making him look every inch the alpha male that he was—the one in charge, the man to whom other men deferred.

As she recognised that fact Louise found herself acknowledging that she wasn't the only one who had grown in the years since Oliver had been conceived. When she looked back now, from the vantage point of her own maturity and awareness, she could judge the more youthful Caesar in a different light. Where then she had seen arrogance and a sense of entitlement, now her expertise obliged her to ask herself if his attitude had been in part a protective cloak he had used to cover the fact that he was alone in the world, taking on the role of his father—a role which meant that he had to command the respect of those for whom he was responsible. With men like Aldo Barado ready to challenge him, perhaps even thinking of him as a young upstart who could not fill his father's shoes, she could see that he might have been vulnerable himself in ways that she had been unable to recognise or understand then.

It was a short distance from admitting that to acknowledging that, for Caesar, having the fact that he had taken *her*—a girl already distrusted and disliked by the elders of the village—to bed made public knowledge would have affected the degree of respect his people had for him.

The Caesar she was watching now, however, was a man completely in charge of himself and his destiny. A man who was not afraid to make a decision and to stand by it. A man who was not afraid to elevate an elderly couple who had suffered the most grievous shame to the position he now had.

'They are Falconaris now, by virtue of the fact of my marriage to their granddaughter and the fact that my son is also of their blood,' she heard Caesar telling Aldo. 'Where else should they rest?'

Where indeed? The villagers were impressed, Louise could tell, and wasn't it the truth that she was a little impressed herself? By virtue of having their ashes interred in his family vault Caesar had lifted her grandparents above criticism by anyone. As a modern woman Louise knew she should object to such a traditional and male-dominated attitude, but as her grandparents' grandchild, and knowing how much it would have meant to them, she couldn't. Just as she couldn't deny her maternal pride in Oliver, later in the proceedings, as he carried out his role faultlessly, only having to look once to his father for guidance, the smile and the touch on his arm that Caesar gave him all Ollie needed to enable him to perform his part perfectly.

After the formal ceremony had been completed everyone headed for the village square, where a buffet meal was quickly laid out beneath the ancient olive trees that shaded the square from the hot sun.

The women of the village might be watching her and

no doubt judging her, withholding their assessment of her as Caesar's wife, Louise reflected, but there was no doubt about their reaction to Oliver.

'He is every inch his father's son,' one elderly matriarch announced with obvious approval. 'A Falconari through and through.'

Oliver *was* every inch Caesar's son, it was true, and he was glorying in being with his father.

'They are so happy together,' Anna Maria told Louise, coming to sit with her on one of the ancient wooden benches on the edge of the square, where Louise had gone to sit and watch whilst Caesar moved amongst the villagers, Oliver at his side.

Louise nodded her head. Just watching father and son together, she felt a sense of peace and completeness fill her. No matter what her own feelings, her marriage to Caesar had been the right thing to do for Ollie. Gone was the downbent head, the surly defensiveness. Now he held himself proudly, was loving towards her and protective of her. Now she could see a hint of the man he would one day be under Caesar's careful and loving guidance. Because Caesar *did* love his son, even if he did not love her.

A pain as though someone had turned a knife inside her chest struck her so hard that she actually lifted her hand to place it on her ribs. Where had it come from—and why? She did not *want* Caesar to love her. For her to want that she would have to love him, and she didn't. She mustn't. It was all this resurrecting and dissecting of the past that was responsible, throwing her back into the emotions she had felt then. Emotions that had no place in the present. Emotions it was laughable to think could be real. They were like the early-morning mist that clothed the tops of the distant mountains, creating a landscape that did not really exist. Or was it the other way around?

Had she used necessity to conceal what was really in her heart and what she really felt? Surely not! It was totally ridiculous to think that she had somehow secretly loved Caesar for all these years, her love like some...some inert object frozen in time that had burst into renewed life the minute he was back in her life.

Wasn't it?

'You look a bit pale. Are you all right?'

The shock of Caesar materialising at her side when she was in the grip of such personal and frightening thoughts was enough to have her retreating further into the shadows of the olive tree. Her 'I'm fine,' was so clipped and terse that it had Caesar frowning.

'Well, you don't look it. It's bound to have been a difficult day for you, I know.'

Far more difficult than he realized, and for a very different reason than he meant, Louise admitted inwardly. Yes, the interment of her grandparents' ashes had been very emotional, but there had been a sense of completion of a duty about the proceedings for her, a feeling of a task properly done and a debt repaid which, allied to her pride in Oliver, had lifted her. No, it wasn't the interment of her grandparents' ashes that had left her feeing so weak and alone. It was the danger of the thoughts inside her own head that were refusing to be silenced.

It *had* been a long day, resulting in a faintly nagging headache which was refusing to go away. The boys were already in bed, Oliver having actually fallen asleep mid–happy chatter to her about how much he had learned from Caesar during the day. Now Louise herself was yawning as she made her way from the bathroom towards the bed. Caesar was still downstairs with Anna Maria, discussing a brief trip to Rome to show Ollie something of the city. A tactful means, no doubt, of allowing her to get to bed before he came into the suite. And of course she was relieved that he had done that—just as she was relieved that he hadn't made any attempt to seduce her.

Ultimately, would he take a mistress to answer that need? The white-fire stab of antipathy to that thought that drove into her had her standing frozen by the side of the bed. She minded that much? It was for Oliver's sake, because she did not want her son growing up believing that that kind of behaviour was acceptable. *Liar, liar,* her inner voice returned to mock her.

Her head had started to pound painfully.

She'd give anything for a hot, freshly made cup of tea, Louise acknowledged. There was a small but very well equipped kitchen off the suite's sitting room, which Caesar used to fend for himself when he was working late rather than disturbing his staff.

His consideration for those who worked for him had been another eye-opener, Louise admitted as she pulled on the silk robe that matched the beautifully simple and elegant silk nightgown she was wearing, and then crossed the sitting room floor in the direction of the kitchen.

Initially, when Anna Maria had announced that Caesar had instructed her to ask some of Italy's top designers to send a selection of clothes to the *castello* for Louise to choose from, Louise had been tempted to refuse to wear them. She had her own clothes, after all. But then she had reminded herself of the new role she was going to have to play, the new 'job' that she had in effect taken on—a job for which she would be required to dress as appropriately as she had for her previous job. She had been sparing in her choice of clothes, though, and it had been Anna Maria who had included the beautifully made lingerie which now filled several drawers in Louise's dressing room closets.

A quick inspection of the kitchen cupboards revealed that someone had thought to stock them with proper English teabags. Just the thought of that soothing brew was almost enough to smooth away some of the tension of her headache, and five minutes later, sipping the hot, welcome brew as she left the kitchen on her way back to her bedroom, she gave a small sigh of pleasure—only to come to an abrupt halt when the suite door opened and Caesar came in.

It was obvious from his frown that her presence in 'his' part of the suite wasn't welcome to him.

'I'm sorry,' Louise apologised. 'I just wanted a cup of tea.' She started to walk faster, skirting round him as she forced herself to add, 'Thank you for what you did today for my grandparents.'

'I didn't do it for them.'

Caesar's voice was curt, as though the words had been forced out of him against his will and represented an admission of some inner weakness he had not wanted to make. But that was impossible. Caesar would never allow himself to be forced to do or say anything he didn't want to do or say.

Why had he said that? Did he really want her to know of his weakness? That his decision to have the Falconari crypt opened and her grandparents' ashes interred there had been something he'd done for *her*? Why? To make amends for the past or because he wanted to please her? Because he wanted… Because he wanted her?

Had she really been foolish enough to think that it had been consideration for her grandparents that had motivated him? If so, she should have known better, Louise recognized.

'No, I don't suppose you did,' she said, every bit as clipped as his own declaration had been. 'It's the Falconari name, the Falconari status that matters to you, after all—not my grandparents.'

'I have to think of Oliver,' was all Caesar could allow himself to say.

'He is so very much your son.' The words were dragged from her. 'I lost count of the number of people who said as much to me today.'

'He has you to thank for the loving upbringing he has had.'

A compliment? From Caesar?

The shock of recognising that it was had her admitting truthfully, 'I didn't want him to suffer as I did during my own childhood. I wanted him to feel secure in my love and not to ever have to worry about losing it.'

'Is that why there hasn't been a man—a lover—in your life?'

Louise took a quick drink of her tea in an attempt to conceal the shock she felt. How could he possibly know that?

'I don't have to answer that question,' she told him, continuing to head for the bedroom.

'But it is the truth. There hasn't been any other man for you, either before me or after me.'

It was a statement, not a question, and one that was making her feel very vulnerable indeed, desperate to escape from him. But why? Her decision to live a sexless, partnerless life hadn't been made because of him but because of Oliver.

When Louise didn't say anything, Caesar told her, 'After I learned about Oliver I instigated certain enquiries...'

'You paid someone to investigate me? To rifle through

my private life like…as though they were going through my dirty washing?'

Louise's angry revulsion filled her voice. He had wanted to please, but instead she was reacting as though he had insulted her.

'I had no choice,' Caesar defended himself. 'A man in my position…'

'Oh, yes, of course—your position… Of course that must take precedence over everything and everyone else.'

'Not for my sake,' Caesar insisted, 'but for the sake of my people. Oliver will be their *Duca* after my death.'

'Yes, I know that.' Louise stopped him, putting down her teacup as she turned to confront him. 'But I want more for my son than a hereditary title. The only reason I have agreed to this sham marriage and this whole charade is because I want Oliver to have the parenting, the bond with his father that—'

'That you never had. I understand that. And I promise you that Oliver will never, ever have to question either my love for him or my responsibility towards him. I think you know and believe that yourself, without me having to state it, because I know enough about you to know that you would never have agreed to allowing me into your lives if you did not.'

'I don't recall there being much choice for me! You threatened to take Oliver from me if I didn't agree.'

'He is my son.'

'*Our* son,' she corrected him, but even as she did so Louise knew that Caesar was right.

Oliver was his son, and that fact had already been brought home to her in the short time that father and son had already been together. Oliver had gravitated quickly to Caesar; he looked up to him, laughed and joked with him, shared a male intimacy with him that showed her over and over again just how close the bond between them already was. She could never take Oliver from Caesar now. She knew that. But she was still angry. Very angry.

'And what else did you learn from these enquiries you instigated?' she challenged him. 'Enquiries which I presume you made to prove that I wasn't a fit mother for Oliver.'

If that had originally been what he had hoped that hope had been sent packing for ever by the rush of compassion and guilt he had felt when he had read in the reports the truth about her.

'What I learned,' he told her truthfully, 'was that I was guilty of an unforgivable error of judgement. I learned that your father had treated you very badly, and that his treatment of you was responsible for your own reaction to it and to me.'

Simple words, but oh, how they still had the power to hurt as they resurrected the fear that had dominated her childhood: that somehow it was *her* fault that her parents didn't love her, that it was a flaw in *her* that was to blame. You could teach yourself via counselling and education to untangle the knotted misery of a painful past, but somehow those knots, even when undone, left a discernible kink that could always be seen and felt by those who knew where to look for it.

'I don't want your pity,' she told him fiercely. 'There is never merely one person to blame in a family which is dysfunctional. As you no doubt know, my father resented being forced into marriage and parenthood. No wonder he rejected me.'

The look in her eyes defied him to argue with her. She had so much pride, so much strength, and yet at the same time she was so vulnerable. Caesar could feel within himself the intensity of his desire to reach out to her, to tell her...

What? That he wanted them to give their marriage a proper chance? That he wanted her? That he had never forgotten her? That a part of him had been left raw with its longing for her even though he had fought fiercely to deny that reality?

Oblivious to Caesar's private thoughts, and wrapping her pride around herself as protection—after all it wasn't just her father who had rejected her, was it?—Louise carried on.

'Perhaps if I'd behaved better, been a different and more appealing child instead of being so difficult and making him ashamed of me, things might have been different.'

Old habits died hard, and despite her training Louise knew that she had automatically fallen into her old familiar role of protecting her father at her own expense. Caesar would agree with her definition, of course. She could remember the look of male anger and embarrassment he had exchanged with her father that fateful morning: two men sharing their wish not to be involved with her.

'Your father's shame should be for himself. Where you are concerned he has a great deal to be ashamed of. And so do I.'

The terse, harsh words of condemnation had Louise turning to look directly at Caesar. Such a declaration was the last thing she had expected to hear from him, and it confused her, making her feel both defensive and at the same time filling her with a dangerous, aching longing to believe that he genuinely cared about what had happened to her—even though she knew he did not.

'I...I don't want to talk about it any more.'

The truth was that she couldn't trust herself to speak about it any more in case she gave herself away. Turning away from Caesar, she headed for the open doors to the bedroom, but Caesar stopped her, moving to stand in front of her and blocking her exit.

'Louise.'

She could feel his heart beating. This close to him she was so conscious of everything about him—especially all those things she didn't want to be conscious of: his maleness and her own vulnerability to it, the scent of his skin, the ache deep down in her own body caused by his proximity.

She tried to push past him but he stopped her, taking hold of her, and then she was in his arms and he was kissing her fiercely, determinedly—almost as though he was laying claim to her. And she was kissing him back, letting him draw her so close to him that she could feel the hard muscles of his thighs and his arousal, letting him slide his hands beneath her robe to caress her naked back where her satin nightgown dipped down low.

Such a hunger possessed her—such a need, such an aching, tearing, irresistible yearning that she couldn't withstand its call. Beneath the hot, hard pressure of his kiss her lips parted, her tongue eagerly seeking the remembered sensuality of his, her whole body shuddering with remembered pleasure when his tongue probed deeply into the soft cavern of her mouth. The dull ache low down in her body flared into the same pulsing urgency she could feel throbbing through Caesar's erection. She wanted to hold him, to touch him, to own him as she had done all those years ago. She wanted to caress his flesh with her fingertips and her lips, and she wanted him to caress her in the same way.

A need it was impossible for her to control had come

out of nowhere to crush all the opposition in its way. Everything she had believed she had learned was forgotten as the desire only he could arouse within her took control.

'Louise.'

How sweetly savage and filled with longing her name sounded on his lips—as though she were the only woman he wanted, the only woman he could ever want. It was a sound that fed the out-of-control flames of her own longing.

He was pushing her robe off her shoulders, sliding down one of the straps of her nightgown, kissing his way along the slope of her shoulder whilst his fingertips teased the erect crest of her exposed breast. It had been nearly ten years since he had last touched her, and yet her body remembered every single sensation he had aroused in it then as faithfully as if he had imprinted that memory upon her.

The sensation of his mouth covering her nipple drew a sharp cry of driven pleasure from her. *This* was what she had both feared and longed for so much—these feelings and Caesar. Only Caesar. And now it was too late to stop what was happening, what she wanted to happen so much, Louise acknowledged.

When Caesar released her nipple to look deeply into her eyes, she reached for him, unfastening the buttons on his shirt, making small mewling sounds of pleasure at the feel of his hot male flesh beneath her touch—a tentative touch at first, but one that quickly grew bolder when she saw the tension in his jaw and heard the groan of arousal he was fighting to suppress. It was only fair that he should experience what she was experiencing, that he should ache for her and long for her as she was doing for him. It was only fair that she should ramp up the sensual tension between him, pleasuring herself with her avid hunger for the sight and the feel of him.

A hot, immediate surge of responsiveness to him took her senses right down to the depths of her own desire for him, urging her to hurry, to enjoy what she could of him before he rejected her all over again. The voice inside her was urging her towards caution, warning her that she could only be hurt. She ignored it. Her body ruthlessly crushed anything that threatened to stand in the way of satisfaction of the need it had suppressed for so very long.

It was instinct and not experience that had her leaning forward to trace the line of his collarbone with her lips, her whole body trembling as she breathed the aphrodisiacal scent of his naked flesh. Boldly she let her hands skim his torso and then rest on his belt, her heartbeat skyrocketing as slowly, centimetre by centimetre, she gave in to the urge possessing her to know him more intimately. After all he could choose to stop her if he wished—but he wasn't doing so.

And then she forgot all about him stopping her, forgot about everything apart from the agonising tug on her own deep inner sexuality caused by what she was doing. Beneath her fingertips the dark arrowing of his intimate body hair felt unexpectedly silky soft, and the erection she could see was thick and hard, its pulse mirroring the pulse dominating her own body.

'Caesar…'

It was no more than a whispered breath but it was enough, because he was reaching for her, carrying her to the bed, tugging off his own clothes and hers to leave them both naked, clothed only in the sensual heat of their mutual need.

His kiss took her mouth, possessing it, drawing from her the sweetness of a response she couldn't withhold.

His hand cupped her breasts, shaping them and tormenting her, until she made a sound of fierce female longing deep in her throat.

In response Caesar lifted his mouth from hers to tease tiny kisses along the line of her throat and behind her ear, where his touch made her shudder and call out to him. Then he moved down along her shoulder and her breast, his tongue tormenting the already almost too sensitised flesh of her nipple with its sensually rough pleasuring.

When she protested, 'No! I can't bear it any more!' Caesar looked up at her.

'Now you know how I felt when you touched me earlier,' he told her in a voice thick with male arousal. 'Now you know how much you aroused me and how much I want you.'

He was kissing his way down along her body. Already her sex was swollen and wet, but now it pulsed urgently and wantonly, causing her to place her hand over it in an instinctive attempt to calm and silence it.

There was no point, though. Caesar was already kissing her there through her spread fingers, nibbling erotically at the sensually vulnerable flesh of her thighs.

The increase in her own hot, wet heat made her cry out, unable either to protest or resist when Caesar removed her hand and then spread open the outer lips of her sex.

How could such a light, delicate touch from his fingertips evoke such an intense, out-of-control response that had her crying out to him, her body writhing in his hold beneath the onslaught of pleasure he was giving her? How could he take that pleasure even higher—so much higher that she cried out again helplessly and begged him not to make her endure any more of it without relief and release? She felt the stroke of his tongue-tip between the open wet lips of her sex to her clitoris, and he ignored her cries to draw from her a climax so intense that it claimed every last bit of her. Just as he had claimed *her*, and her love.

Her love. She loved Caesar.

She loved him so much.

Instantly Louise froze, and then frantically pushed Caesar away, her hand trembling as she reached for her clothes, ignoring him as she fled to the privacy of her bathroom, locking the door behind her and then leaning on that door, her heart pounding so painfully fast that she thought it might burst out of her chest wall.

Now, when it was too late, a terrible sick awareness of her own danger was filling her. She must not love him. She should never have allowed him to so much as touch her, let alone take her to bed. If she hadn't fled from him now she would have ended up humiliating herself again by telling him that she loved him, she knew.

From the other side of the locked door she could hear Caesar calling her name, insisting that she come out of the bathroom.

'No,' she told him. 'You shouldn't have touched me. That wasn't part of our bargain.'

She was right, Caesar knew, but right now he was aching so damn much for her that the intensity of his need shocked him. And he hadn't been the only one to experience it.

'You wanted me as much as I wanted you,' he insisted.

'No,' Louise denied, even though she knew that she was lying.

It was true. She still loved Caesar. Or rather she had fallen in love with the man he had become. But loving Caesar made her vulnerable, because he did not love her.

In the bedroom Caesar picked up the robe Louise had left behind, the scent of her body filling his nostrils as he did so. His body was a raw, raging storm of need for her—and she had wanted him too, even if she now denied it.

Wanted him, but nothing more than that. Caesar was desperately afraid that it was something much more than sexual desire that he felt for Louise and wanted from her. And that something was love. The love he had denied for years that he could feel for her. The love he could no longer deny.

CHAPTER NINE

'ARE you sure you won't change your mind and come with us all to Rome, Louise? It isn't too late. We can delay our departure whilst you pack.'

It was two o'clock in the afternoon and they were all gathered in the hallway, the boys, Anna Maria, her husband and Caesar, on the point of leaving for the airport where a private jet was waiting to transport them to Rome for a for brief three-day trip.

'No, I really can't,' Louise answered Anna Maria. 'I've got some files to prepare and send to London.'

It wasn't a total lie, but Louise knew that her late employers were in reality happy to give her as much time as she needed to write her final reports. The reality was that she didn't want to join the trip to Rome because of Caesar. It would mean her being in close proximity to him, both during the journey to Rome and during the visit itself, even if Caesar *had* booked hotel accommodation for the three of them.

Whilst Caesar might be able to play the part of a loving and happy new husband in public, without the small intimacies that would involve having any discernible effect on him, the same certainly wasn't true for her. Every time he was merely within arm's length of her, her body started reacting as though it was possessed by a force neither she nor it could control. In a sense it was. And that force was love. Had she *really* only agreed to marry Caesar for Ollie's sake? What if the emotions that had kept themselves hidden had had a secret agenda all along? Like going wild in Caesar's arms when he had kissed her and touched her. What a clever idea *that* had been, destroying her peace of mind and putting her in a position where she was now mortally afraid that Caesar's merest touch might re-ignite the smouldering embers of the need that she had tried and was still trying to quell.

How shameful it was that she should feel like this about him—every bit as shameful as it had been to be misjudged and then rejected by him. Never again did she want to be that girl she had once been, pleading with him to want her and to love her. She had Ollie to think of now.

Oh, Caesar might take her to bed—when he didn't have anything better to do—but she wanted more than that. She wanted his love.

It was obvious that he wasn't pleased by her refusal to accompany them to Rome. Louise had a strong suspicion from the grim look he was giving her right now that he knew that she was making an excuse not to go because of him. But did he know *why* she felt she needed to make that excuse? Louise profoundly hoped not.

It might only be a handful of days since she had made the shocking, heart-stopping discovery that she loved him, but those three days had been an agony of torment and dread as she did everything she could to keep as much distance between them as possible.

Her behaviour on the night of her discovery had shown her just how vulnerable she was to his physical presence and his physical touch. She could not trust herself not to give away her feelings—just as she could not trust herself not to respond to him should he choose to touch her again. How had it happened? How had it come about that she had fallen in love with him and that she was now spending her nights lying awake in her bed—*his* bed— aching with longing for him and at the same time filled with a dread of revealing that need to him because she knew that he would never return her love?

'Well, if you're sure…'

'I'm sure,' Louise confirmed to Caesar's cousin, returning her affectionate hug and then feeling her heart soften when Ollie came over to her and hugged her as well. He was at that age now when he was normally embarrassed by public displays of maternal love, but she had noticed how much more physically affectionate he had become towards her since Caesar had come into his life.

'I'm sorry you aren't going to be with us, Mum,' he told her.

'It will be good for you and your father to have some time together,' Louise said truthfully, making herself smile reassuringly.

'Very noble,' Caesar murmured wryly when it was his turn to say his goodbyes to her. 'Or at least it would be if it wasn't perfectly clear to me that you're motivated more by keeping your distance from me than giving me and Oliver time together.'

'Do you blame me?'

'Because I showed you that you are a woman as well as a mother?'

'Oh, you two, it's obvious you're newly married. Look at the two of you whispering sweet nothings to one another,' Anna Maria teased them.

Caesar was bending his head towards her, his hands on her upper arms keeping her imprisoned and motionless. His kiss was light, the mere brush of his lips against hers, but still her mouth trembled beneath it and she had to fight to stop herself parting her lips, inviting him to kiss her more intimately and winding her arms around his neck to pull him closer.

If he didn't let her go now he'd end up picking her up and carrying her to his bed, Caesar acknowledged, and once he had her there, making love to her until she admitted that she wanted him just as much as he wanted her. Instead, however, he forced himself to release Louise and step back from her.

It had shocked him to discover how much he wanted her. Having her in his arms again had taken him straight back to that first time. The fierce, surging need for her was possessing him now just as much as it had done then. Why? Why out of all the women he had known did she have this effect on him? Surely only love could make a man ache and need so much?

Love? He was a mature, rational human being. It was surely impossible that he could have fallen in love with a girl who represented everything he disliked and then gone on loving her without even knowing it for so many years simply because his body had never stopped wanting her?

Was it? Had he forgotten that fierce savage stab of emotion he had felt when he had first read Louise's grandfather's letter? That visceral knowing and wanting what he was reading to be true—and not just because it would mean he would have a son? On the face of it, before he had seen her again, Louise should have been the last woman he wanted to be his son's mother, but what he had felt had been a gut-wrenching rush of joy.

Louise. He turned to look at her but she had already turned away from him, rejecting him as she had done in his bedroom. Rejecting him even though her body had told him that she wanted him.

He took a step towards her, suddenly reluctant to leave,

but then Oliver urged him, 'Come on, Dad,' and he had to turn back to the small group waiting for him.

Determinedly Louise pinned a smile to her face as she stood and waved the two cars away, standing there until they had disappeared from sight.

It was over an hour's drive to the airport. Caesar had Oliver and Anna Maria's son who was closest in age to him in his car, whilst Anna Maria and her husband had the other two boys with them. Oliver had been chattering away happily to Carlo in the back of the car when suddenly Carlo broke off excitedly, to draw Oliver's attention to the dark clouds massing over the mountains behind them.

'Just look at that! It means there's going to be a real storm over the *castello*, doesn't it, Uncle Caesar? With lots of thunder and lightning!'

A brief glance in his driving mirror showed Caesar that Carlo was right, and that the *castello* was likely to be in the path of the storm gathering in the mountains.

'Remember last year when the lightning hit that tree?' Without waiting for Caesar to reply Carlo spoke again to Oliver. 'It was really scary, and Uncle Caesar told us that sometimes lightning strikes the *castello* itself. I'd love to see that, wouldn't you?'

Oliver had gone very pale, even though he managed to nod his head. They had now reached the airport, and as he headed for the reception area for the private jets Caesar frowned. The thought of the storm obviously frightened his son. He wanted to reassure him that it was nothing to worry about and wouldn't affect them—such fierce storms did happen at this time of the year, but only in the mountains—but he didn't want to draw attention to Oliver's fear in front of Carlo.

As soon as he'd stopped the car and made sure it was safe for the boys to get out he drew Oliver to one side, keeping his hand protectively on his shoulder, whilst Carlo joined his parents.

'There's no need to be afraid of the storm, Ollie. It won't affect us,' he said quietly.

'It's not me that gets frightened,' Oliver told him immediately. 'It's Mum. She hates thunder and lightning.'

Louise was frightened by storms and thunder and lightning? The desire Caesar immediately felt to protect her confirmed what he already knew about his feelings for her.

'She'll be perfectly safe in the *castello*. It's been there a very long time and has survived an awful lot of thunderstorms,' he reassured Oliver.

Oliver didn't look reassured, though. His head was bent, the tips of his ears red.

'Mum gets *really* scared, though. She tries to pretend that she isn't but I know that she is. Because I saw her once when…'

'When what, Ollie?'

His son was looking so anxious and upset that Caesar knew he needed to get to the bottom of his concern—and all the more so because it involved Louise.

'I'm not supposed to say anything. Mum doesn't know that I saw her, or that I know, and great-grandad made me promise that I wouldn't, but it's different telling you, isn't it?' Oliver asked, lifting his head to look directly at his father.

'Yes, it *is* different telling me, because it's my responsibility now to look after your mother. Lots of people don't like thunderstorms, you know. It's nothing to feel ashamed about. I can phone the *castello* and make sure that the shutters are closed so that your mother doesn't have to see the storm if you think that will help.'

Oliver shook his head.

'That might make it worse. There was an awful storm in London a couple of years ago and Mum was…she was so afraid… Just shaking and crying, and Great-grandma was sitting with her in her bedroom holding her. Great-grandad told me that Mum wouldn't want me to say anything about it to her. He told me it was because of something that had happened when she was a little girl. Lightning struck a tree in the garden when she was staying with her father and out playing in the garden, so she ran inside to her father, crying. He was angry with her because he was busy, and when she wouldn't stop crying he locked her in a cupboard under the stairs and left her there until the storm was over. Great-grandad said that Mum has been terrified of thunderstorms ever since, and that she hates being alone during them.'

Caesar closed his eyes briefly as he held his son close. What an unbelievably cruel thing to do to a vulnerable, frightened child.

'But Mum won't be alone in the *castello*, will she?'

'No, she won't, Oliver.'

Releasing his son, Caesar went over to his cousin.

'I have to go back to the *castello*,' he told her quickly. 'All of you go on to Rome. Oliver can go with you.'

'You want to persuade Louise to change her mind, don't you?' Anna Maria smiled. 'I could see that you weren't keen on leaving her behind. You go ahead—and don't worry about Oliver. He'll be fine with us.'

Nodding his head, Caesar went back to his son.

'I'm going back to the *castello* to make sure that your mother is all right. You're to go on to Rome with Anna Maria.'

'You won't tell Mum what I told you, will you?' Oliver asked anxiously.

'No, I won't,' Caesar assured him, giving him a fierce hug before heading back to the car.

Ahead of him the storm clouds were banked up on the horizon, darkening the sky, and jagged flashes of lightning accompanied the distant sound of thunder. Although he'd tried telephoning the *castello* there was no reply. It wasn't unusual for these ferocious storms to affect both the power supply and the cell-phone networks. *He* might love the magnificence of such storms, but that didn't mean he couldn't relate to Louise's terror—especially after what Oliver had told him. The more he learned about her father the greater his angry contempt for the other man grew.

Just thinking about the fear Louise must be experiencing had him pressing down harder on the accelerator pedal of his car.

The storm seemed to come out of nowhere, the clear blue of the sky turning grey and then black over the mountains, but it wasn't until she heard the first dull rumble of thunder that Louise really started to feel afraid.

Apprehensive, she moved from room to room, her attention drawn to each window—especially those with a view of the mountains. Her pulse was racing and the adrenaline of fear was pouring through her body, increasing her heart-rate and drying out her mouth whilst her stomach turned sickening somersaults with nausea.

In the main salon she saw the housekeeper, going the other way.

'I'm just going upstairs for a rest,' she told her.

'I'll make sure that no one disturbs you,' the housekeeper assured her, sighing as another clap of thunder caused her to raise her voice. 'These storms, they are so violent and noisy,' she added, before continuing on her way.

Her fear made her feel ashamed and guilty, Louise acknowledged, just as her father had made her feel all those years ago, when she had run in screaming from his garden after seeing the tree in his garden hit by lightning. Her father had been working, and when she had tried to run to him, wanting to be picked up and held safe in his arms, he had been angry with her, pushing her away and telling her to stop making a fuss. Instead of stopping her panicked tears, his refusal to comfort her, accompanied by another flash of lightning right outside the French windows, had caused her instead to scream out in fear.

She had been half-hysterical when he had lost his temper with her and dragged her to the large cupboard beneath the stairs, pushing her inside and locking the door, telling her that she couldn't come out until she could control herself. Her behaviour, her father had said when he had eventually released her, was ridiculous for a big girl of eight.

The whole experience had left her with not only a terrible fear of thunderstorms but of her own reaction to them. Her father had been so angry with her. She had disgraced herself with her hysterics. She must never, *ever* let herself down like that again. Despite all the counselling she had been given, her fear of her reaction to thunderstorms had been something she'd never been able to conquer. For that reason she tried to avoid them, but if she had to endure one then, ironically, her greatest need was to seek out somewhere dark and enclosed, where she could shut herself away so that no one else could see her fall apart. The only place to shut herself away in the *castello* was Caesar's suite.

It seemed to Louise, as she made her way up the stairs and then along the long gallery with its many sets of windows, that the lightning seemed to leap from window to window, mocking and taunting her as she fought not to give in to her driving instinct to run. She knew that hearing thunder so close at hand, seeing vivid lightning split open the growing stormy darkness of the sky, would not help her, and yet she could not turn away from it. Her gaze was fixed on the spectacle outside, watching the storm grow ever closer.

The sitting room of the suite smelled faintly of Caesar's cologne, and the recognition momentarily distracted her as she breathed it in and tried not to let herself wish that he was here. Not, of course, that Caesar's reaction to her weakness would be any different from her father's. She couldn't imagine Caesar being at all tolerant of such vulnerability.

From the sitting room window Louise saw the lights across the courtyard flutter and then dim, surging back into bright life only to be extinguished by a blinding flash of lightning which pierced the darkness, silvering the room with its metallic light. In the mirror in the sitting room Louise caught sight of her own reflection, her expression reflecting her fear. Soon now the storm would be overhead. Soon she would be reliving that awful moment in the garden when the oak tree had been struck and she had feared that she would be the storm's next victim.

She looked at the bed. Even with the curtains closed she would still be able to see the storm. A new crash of thunder—surely there were only seconds between them now?—galvanised her into instinctively seeking the security she needed by running towards the door to Caesar's dressing room and pulling it open.

Inside the windowless room it would have been completely dark if it hadn't been for the light from the open door, which showed her way to the sofa on which Caesar now slept. Like the sitting room, Caesar's dressing room smelled faintly of his cologne and of him.

Louise had no idea why that should have the effect of both accelerating her pulse and calming her fear; she only knew that, just like Ollie when he had been little and had needed his comfort blanket, she wanted to draw the scent of Caesar close to her for her own comfort.

Closing the door, she picked her way to the sofa in darkness, her legs trembling. The sound of another thunderclap, this one surely almost overhead, froze her to the spot where she was standing. Then she curled up in a small terrified ball when the noise had stopped, releasing her from her terrified imprisonment.

Caesar cursed beneath his breath. Even the powerful windscreen wipers of his car were unable to cope fully with the pouring rain.

Lightning illuminated the dark, unlit bulk of the *castello*, its lightless windows picked out by his headlights as Caesar pulled up in front of the entrance.

In the hallway he found his housekeeper, instructing some of the staff to get the generator working and others to start lighting candles. If she was surprised to see him she didn't show it.

'My wife,' Caesar asked, 'where is she?'

'In your suite, Your Excellency. She said that she wanted to rest and that she wasn't to be disturbed.'

Because she didn't want anyone else to witness her fear, Caesar recognised as he took the stairs two at a time. He felt as though someone had closed a fist around his heart and was squeezing it hard as he thought of what it must have been like to be that child, terrified by a violent

storm and punished for that fear by the person she had
turned to for understanding and comfort.

If only all those years ago he had known about her
what he knew now. If only he had had the wisdom, the
insight, the compassion to look beyond the obvious and
see the person she really was.

As he raced along the portrait gallery lightning was
striking just beyond the *castello*, and the noise of the
thunder was deafening. Soon the storm would be fully
overhead.

He had reached the suite. He pushed open the door,
cursing himself for not thinking to bring some form of
light with him as he moved from the sitting room to the
bedroom, his eyes adjusting to the darkness and his heart
plunging in anxiety as he saw the smooth, untouched
emptiness of the bed.

Where *was* she? She sought out dark, safe places,
Oliver had said.

Caesar strode over to the door to Louise's dressing
room, its emptiness revealed by the stuttering flicker of
the power returning as the generator kicked in. Like her
dressing room, the bathroom too was empty.

Where *was* she?

Fear for her gripped him by the throat. If he had
needed any further proof of just how he felt about her,
just how much she mattered to him, just how much he
loved her, then everything he had felt from the moment
Oliver had told him about her fear of storms had provided it. There was no way he could hide from the truth
now, and no way he wanted to. All he wanted was to find
Louise and tell her that she was safe, that he would hold
her and love her and protect her for as long as he lived,
and that she would never, ever again have to fear reaching out to someone only to be rejected.

But first he had to find her.

He returned to the bedroom and then came to an abrupt halt as he saw a thin light shining beneath the door to his own dressing room. *His* dressing room? Surely the last place she would go to seek refuge—just as he was the last person she would turn to. But he knew he hadn't left that light on. Something—a small glimmer of hope, a small surge of joy like the fluttering of a candle in the wind—trembled within him.

He pushed open the door.

She was lying curled up in a tight little ball on the sofa, covered in one of his jackets, so that all he could really see of her was her legs and a few strands of blonde hair that weren't covered by the jacket she had pulled up around herself.

An aching, an almost unbearable, sharply sweet sense of humility and love filled him.

He waited until he had reached her and crouched down beside her before reaching out to place his hand on her tense body and say her name softly.

The lightning was so close to the thunder now. She could hear them even here, in this protected window-less room. It could only be seconds before the storm was right overhead. The temptation to take one of Caesar's jackets from his closet and wrap it around her had been one she couldn't resist. The comfort of the scent of his cologne and of Caesar himself was a wretched treach-ery that somehow brought her a warped kind of pleasure.

For it to somehow produce Caesar's *voice*, though, was impossible and must surely mean that she was going mad. Caesar couldn't possibly be here. But she wanted him to be here, didn't she? She wanted that more than anything else in the world. Weak tears burned her eyes.

The sudden explosion of flashes of lightning she could

see illuminating the bedroom from the door that Caesar had left open, followed by thunder right overhead drove every other thought out of her head. Her sharp cry of terror and her rigid body caused Caesar to reach for her, sitting on the sofa next to her as he drew her trembling body into his arms.

She felt incredibly fragile, her whole body trembling from head to foot. Such strong emotion swept him that he had to bend his head to blink away the feelings dampening his eyes. How could he have ever allowed himself to think that she didn't matter? How could he ever have allowed himself to turn his back on her and publicly condemn her? His own hands trembled as he held her beneath the force of his own remorse and regret.

Another crack of thunder overhead had her burrowing closer to him with a small sound of terror.

'It's all right, Lou. It's all right. Everything's going to be all right.'

Caesar. He was here. And he had seen her hysteria and her weakness. He had witnessed what she had promised herself no one else would ever witness.

A soft moan of despair tore at her throat as she tried to pull away from him, but Caesar was refusing to let her go, ignoring her attempts to break free of him and instead binding her even closer to him—so close that her face was pressed against his throat, her lips to his bare flesh. It would be the easiest thing in the world to kiss that column of warm, bare, beloved Caesar flesh.

Now when she trembled violently in his arms it wasn't because of the thunderstorm that was already receding and beginning to die away. Instead it was caused by an even greater threat to her emotional security.

Caesar. Here. Holding her. Keeping her close to him, whispering words that unbelievably suggested that he cared about her. But that was impossible. She only mattered to him because of Oliver.

Her son. Guilt and fear immediately tensed her body.

'Why did you come back? Where's Oliver?' she delivered, in a maternal voice that was openly fearful and anxious as terrifying mental images of the danger the storm might have caused to her son filled her imagination.

'Probably in Rome by now,' Caesar told her. 'And as for why I came back…'

He slid one hand beneath her chin and along her neck, tilting her face up to his own. The touch of his fingertips was so tender and gentle that it locked the breath in her throat.

'I came back because Oliver was very worried about you when he saw that a storm was gathering over the mountains.'

When Louise sucked in her breath he continued.

'You mustn't be cross with him, Louise, I made him tell me how thunderstorms affect you—and why.'

He could feel the jolt of emotion that ran through her as she tried to pull away from him.

'No, don't hide yourself away from me. I am the one who should feel shame, not you. Your father did a very cruel thing, but in my way I have been equally cruel and I have let you down just as badly. Instead of listening to my deepest and truest emotions all those years ago, when we first met, I allowed pride and arrogance, the way I believed I should feel and behave as *Duca* to direct my behaviour rather than what I really felt. Because of that I lost you—a punishment I deserved—and you were hurt, and for that I can never forgive myself.'

'I don't want to discuss this,' Louise told him wildly.

He was probing too deeply, touching places that were too raw, revealing emotions that she knew could so easily betray her. His very gentleness towards her was undermining what was left of her defences.

'We must if we are to have any hope of laying down new foundations for a loving and happy future together.'

Loving?

Even as her eyes widened Caesar was saying softly, 'And that is what we both want, isn't it, Louise? A future based on love?'

She was trapped. Her love for him was obvious and now he pitied her for it—just as he pitied her for her weakness during thunderstorms. There could be no other explanation. She had to defend herself. She had to make him understand that despite her love for him she still had her pride—still wanted Oliver to grow up believing that her sex could be strong and empowered by their emotions, not imprisoned and weakened by them.

'Just because I love you...' she began shakily, but before she could get any further, Caesar interrupted her.

His voice cracked with such raw male emotion that it caught at her own breath, as he said, 'You love me? I had hardly dared... I have no right... I had dreamed and begun to hope. Oh, my love. My sweet, precious love...'

What was happening? Her thoughts were in turmoil, her heart pounding with a mix of exhilaration, hope and disbelief, and then Caesar was kissing her gently, sweetly, with the tender kisses her young self might have yearned for, as he cupped her face and brushed his lips over hers.

This was surely a dream. It had to be. But she knew she could not possibly have dreamed the firm reality of Caesar's broad strong shoulders beneath her hands as she clung to him any more than she could have dreamed the emotion in his voice when he had called her his 'sweet, precious love,' but how could this be? How could it be happening?

'Caesar?' She spoke his name uncertainly beneath his kiss.

Immediately Caesar heard and felt her confusion and her doubt, and equally immediately reacted to it as he forced himself to stop kissing her. He couldn't make himself let her go, though, holding her close, keeping his arms wrapped around her so that her head nestled naturally against his shoulder.

'There is so much I want to say to you,' he told her. 'So much I need to say. So many apologies I need to make, so many pleas for your forgiveness, and it is my hope that we shall have a lifetime together in which I can make those apologies and prove to you how much I love you. How much I have loved you right from the start.'

Louise's sound of denial was accompanied by an attempt to move away from him, but Caesar wouldn't let her. His arms were constraining her with the greatest tenderness and care. He never again wanted her to feel that she wasn't valued or respected or loved in all the ways there were.

'Yes, I know what you must be thinking. All those years ago I behaved towards you with unforgivable cruelty. That cruelty was born of conceit and arrogance. It was the behaviour of a coward too—a man who could not and would not face the truth within himself that he already knew because that truth did not fit the pattern he had drawn for himself. Of all the offences against you of which I am guilty, refusing to acknowledge that I was falling in love with you—even to myself—was the worst. And I *was* falling in love with you, Louise. Something about you burned away everything I thought I knew about myself and the life I had planned for myself. You were not...'

'The kind of girl you wanted to want?' Louise supplied for him.

Caesar exhaled. 'Yes. And because of that I allowed myself to believe the judgements others had made on you instead of making my own. Again I was a coward, because I chose the easier path. Their judgement made it easier for me to deny what I knew I really felt. You gave your sweet self and your love to me and I let you, and then I publicly and cruelly rejected you—because that was what other people expected of me. I can never forgive myself for that.'

Louise could hear the honesty in his voice.

'I don't blame you for what you did, Caesar,' she told him, surprised herself to discover that it was true. 'After all I wasn't honest with you myself. Initially I planned to use you to gain my father's love. It was only later that I—'

When she broke off Caesar prompted her. 'It was only later that you fell in love with me?'

Louise looked away from him. Even now, even knowing that he knew the truth, it was still hard for her to say the words that would leave her vulnerable and afraid. Rejection did that to you over time. It stole away all the belief you might once have had in yourself.

'Louise, look at me—please.'

Caesar was turning her head towards his own, and automatically she lifted her gaze to his, gasping out loud when she saw the pain and the longing so clearly revealed in his eyes. Did it matter to him so much? Did she matter to him so much?

Before she could lose her courage she answered quickly, 'Yes, it was later when I fell in love with you.'

'And I destroyed that love—the most precious gift that can ever be given. Don't think that I didn't suffer because of that. In my dreams and in my most private thoughts you were always there, your memory tormenting me, and today I knew I had to be here with you.'

'You came back because of me? You put me first?' Everything that knowledge made her feel was revealed in her voice.

'Yes. And that's something I should have done a long, long time ago.'

'It hurt me so much when you rejected me.'

'I know. It was unforgivable. And all the more so when what I really wanted to reject and deny was the way you made me feel.'

She looked at him.

'I wanted you so badly, Louise. So very badly. I resented that wanting and I resented you for being the cause of it. It went against everything I believed being a Falconari meant. I was young—and arrogant. More than anything else I hope you will give me a second chance to prove how strong my love for you really is—a second chance to be worthy of your love.'

'Oh, Caesar.'

All that she felt for him was contained in those two words—a simple acknowledgement of her love for him.

'The storm is over,' he told her, looking towards the bedroom. 'Come and look.' Taking hold of her hand, he led the way from the dressing room to the bedroom. Outside it was now growing dark, but it was still possible to see that the sky was clear, and the moon was coming up to illuminate the now storm-free mountains.

'Caesar?'

As she said his name Caesar turned to her, bending his head to kiss her and then picking her up and carrying her towards the bed.

'One storm is over, but there is another, I think, that

is possessing us both with an equal ferocity of need—if you trust me with that need, with our love?'

Could she? Did she trust him? Did she trust herself to take such a risk after everything that had happened? Did she have the courage to trust him and herself?

There was only one way in which she could find out.

Louise looked at him and nodded her head.

'Yes,' she whispered. Her voice grew more fervent as she told him, 'Yes. Caesar. Yes, I do.'

Louise knew what Caesar was asking. She knew too that he understood her answer. When he turned her in his arms and started to kiss her, slowly at first and then with growing passion, she responded to him with a passion of her own—a passion that had been locked away inside her for far too long.

Louise could feel its power and its danger. She could feel herself being swept away by it. For a few seconds her old fear of rejection returned. But, as though he knew what she was thinking and feeling, Caesar held her tight, whispering against her ear.

'It's all right. It's all right. I love you and I'll never let you down again. Just hold on to me, Louise, and I'll keep you safe.'

Safe? When he was making her feel the way she was feeling? When he was making her want to abandon herself completely to him?

'I want you so much.' She couldn't say anything more but she didn't need to. Caesar was sliding her clothes from her body and then covering it with kisses, making her shudder from head to foot when he caressed her eager, melting naked flesh.

From somewhere she found the courage to match her own desire and started to undress him, trembling-fingered, tugging on buttons and male clothing with giddy pleasure as she explored his body with her hands and her mouth. The sensation of the hair-roughened texture of his skin beneath her hands made her quiver with increased need and increased boldness as she explored the taut muscles of his thighs. She had thought him already impressively hard and aroused, but beneath her caress his erection pulsed so fiercely and commandingly that her heartbeat increased to match its demand.

'I want you so much too…'

He had said that to her before—all those years ago.

'Too much?' she asked him, repeating the other words he had said to her then.

Caesar shook his head as he drew her up beside him so that their naked bodies lay together. 'Where my love for you is concerned there could never be anything such as too much.'

Such healing words, such loving words—the words of a man a woman must know she could trust with her own love.

Now was the time for her to cross the final chasm that separated her from the darkness of her past to the present, and the future she knew she wanted.

'I love you, Caesar,' she told him, and then gasped as he kissed her with such an intensity of passion that she knew beyond any shadow of doubt just how much her words meant to him.

Now, in his fervency, he was letting her see his own vulnerability, his own need for her. Beneath his passionate touch, the full, proud flood of her love for him filled her. His expression as he looked down at her body made her shudder with need, made her breasts swell with longing into, soft, rounded spheres of sensuality. A million aroused nerve-endings were cloaked in honey-warm skin, every single one of them urgently responding to his hands and then his lips as he gave her what his ardent look had promised.

But then it was his turn to shudder with mute pleasure as he drew her nipple into his mouth, and she arched against him, wild and wanton, her response feeding his own desire and burning away the last of his self-control.

How often in his dreams and his private, secret imaginings had he longed for her and for this? A lifetime of times, or so it had sometimes felt, but now she was here, and she was his, willingly and with love.

When he parted her thighs she looked up at him, her eyes luminous with her feelings. Her sex was swollen and wet, the slow, erotic caress of his fingertips causing her to draw in her breath and then release it on a wild shudder of pleasure.

'Caesar…'

Louise couldn't bear to wait any longer. She reached up to him, pulling him down against her, quivering with expectation, wrapping her legs around him, gasping out loud. He couldn't wait any longer. He knew her already, and moving into her felt like coming home to a sweetness and a welcome ceaselessly longed for.

They moved together, silently at first and then with growing cries of pleasure, as they abandoned themselves to one another on their journey to that place where for a few seconds out of time they were one perfect whole.

Later, wrapped protectively in Caesar's arms, Louise freely told him of her love for him.

'I don't deserve you,' Caesar whispered back emotionally, 'but I shall strive to do so. I promise you that. My biggest regret, aside from the hurt I have caused you, is the fact that I cannot give you any more children.' His voice became muffled as he buried his face in her hair.

'You have given me Oliver, and you have given me

your love—I could not want for anything else,' Louise assured him truthfully.

She could hear and feel his deep unsteady breath, and for the first time she sensed something of what it must mean to him to have to judge himself as less than the man he had believed himself to be, the man he had been brought up to think of himself as being. Tenderly she wrapped her arms around him, holding him as gently as if he were their son.

When he had himself back under control, he said gruffly, 'I wonder if perhaps there isn't something that directs our lives? Fate—call it what you will—and that something made sure that Oliver would be conceived, so that we would have our second chance to find one another. You are my love and you always will be.'

'Just as you are mine and always will be,' Louise told him back.

A tender kiss, gently exchanged, the sudden silver beam of moonlight on a sensual male torso, and then the curve of an inviting female breast, an upwelling of mutual shared desire, and they were reaching for one another again, whispering precious words of love to one another, knowing that the past had finally been laid to rest.

EPILOGUE

Eighteen months later.

'Just look at Caesar and Ollie showing off Francesca to everyone. I don't think I have ever seen a prouder pair of males.' Anna Maria laughed as she spoke to Louise and the two of them watched father and son introducing Ollie's four-month-old baby sister to the guests invited to her christening.

Their special miracle, as Caesar had described her emotionally when they had looked at the scan together and received the news that, against all the odds, Louise was pregnant. Although a recent check-up had revealed that Caesar's chances of conceiving were extremely low, rather than impossible, neither of them had expected it.

'Sometimes it does happen, when all the probabilities are against it,' the consultant had told them both. 'There is no scientific evidence to explain exactly why, or what makes the difference. I suggest you simply think of it as a gift of happenstance.'

'It is *you* who has made this possible,' Caesar had told her in a raw, unsteady voice once they were on their own, his eyes filled with tears of joy and love. 'You, with your love and with everything that you are.'

'Of course I shall have to look after her when she starts

to grow up—'cos that's what you do when you have a sister, isn't it, Papa?' Louise heard Ollie telling Carlo importantly as Caesar brought Francesca back to her.

'It is indeed,' Caesar confirmed, ruffling his son's hair before both boys went off with Anna Maria to find her other sons and her husband.

The main salon of the *castello* was busy with their guests, but as Caesar handed Francesca back to her, Louise felt as she had done after their daughter's birth, when they had been alone in her hospital room: filled with love and with joy and with the specialness of the connection they shared through the birth of this second child.

Her thoughts moved to her mother, whom she'd invited to the christening. She'd received back one of her usual vague e-mails, filled with promises of a visit that would certainly never come. However, her mother *had* mentioned a present she was going to send for Francesca, and good wishes for the future, and Louise found herself able to look with more compassion than before upon a woman who had never wanted to be a mother.

'Your father's here.'

Caesar's quiet words foreshadowed her thoughts and made Louise's heart thump against her chest wall.

When her father had written to her just before Francesca's birth, to tell her that his marriage to Melinda was over and that she'd walked out on him for someone younger, she hadn't really wanted to know. It had been Caesar who had counselled that perhaps it was time to lay the ghosts of the past to rest.

'He is Ollie's grandfather and your father, Lou. And, reading between the lines of his letter, he is feeling very alone and vulnerable.'

It went against her training to protest that her father had never cared much about leaving *her* alone and vulnerable—and besides, now she was wrapped in the protection of Caesar's love and the happiness of their family life, the misery of her childhood seemed to belong to another faraway life that had no bearing on her current happiness.

Urged on by Caesar, she had written back to her father, offering him her sympathy. Slowly, over the intervening weeks and then months, they had continued their correspondence even if it had been tentative and wary. When taxed, her father had admitted to withholding Caesar's letter from her—at Melinda's insistence. He had begged Louise to allow him to meet his grandson and his son-in-law, reminding her that they were now all the family he had. She hadn't really wanted to agree, but somehow or other she had found herself inviting him to Francesca's christening, followed by a stay at the *castello*.

So far, though, she hadn't really spoken to him very much. She'd had the excuse of the christening, after all. But now, with him looking across the room towards her, a man broken in many ways by the humility forced on him by the defection of his wife, she felt pity for him touch her. Without really making any conscious plan to do so she found that she was walking towards him, carrying Francesca, and knew without having to look round that Caesar would be shadowing her progress protectively.

When she reached her father she looked up into his face—lined now, and thinner. Here was a man who somehow had never quite achieved all that he might have done. She felt pity for him. How awful to be alone at his age, and emotionally dependent for love on the kindness of the daughter he had always resented.

'Hello, Dad,' she said shakily.

'I dare say you don't really want me here—' he began. Louise shook her head, suddenly sure of what she must do as she looked across the room and saw that Oliver was watching them. Family relationships weren't always straightforward or easy, but they were surely worth working at.

'Where else would you be? We're your family, after all. And, speaking of families, how about saying hello to the newest member of it?'

For a moment she thought that her father was going to turn his back on her, but then Louise saw the tears in his eyes.

'It's all right, Dad,' she told him softly. 'Everything is going to be all right.'

Taking Francesca from her, Caesar held her out to his father-in-law, telling him proudly, 'She's got Lou's looks, thank goodness.'

'Got those looks from my side of the family, Lou did,' Louise heard her father respond in a voice that was slightly rusty. 'Prettiest baby that ever was, I can tell you.'

Already he was rewriting the past, Louise thought ruefully. But she didn't have the heart to challenge him. After all, her heart now—like her love—was given to a man who treasured and valued it. A man she could trust always to put her first. A man who truly loved her.

* * * * *

& *A sneaky peek at next month...*

MODERN™

INTERNATIONAL AFFAIRS, SEDUCTION & PASSION GUARANTEED

My wish list for next month's titles...

In stores from 15th June 2012:

☐ The Secrets She Carried – Lynne Graham

☐ Heart of a Desert Warrior – Lucy Monroe

☐ A Royal World Apart – Maisey Yates

☐ The Count's Prize – Christina Hollis

In stores from 6th July 2012:

☐ To Love, Honour and Betray – Jennie Lucas

☐ Unnoticed and Untouched – Lynn Raye Harris

☐ Distracted by her Virtue – Maggie Cox

☐ The Tarnished Jewel of Jazaar – Susanna Carr

☐ Keeping Her Up All Night – Anna Cleary

Available at WHSmith, Tesco, Asda, Eason, Amazon and Apple

Just can't wait?

Visit us Online

You can buy our books online a month before they hit the shops! **www.millsandboon.co.uk**

0612/01

The World of Mills & Boon®

There's a Mills & Boon® series that's perfec
for you. We publish ten series and with new
titles every month, you never have to wait
long for your favourite to come along.

Blaze®
Scorching hot,
sexy reads

By Request
Relive the romance with
the best of the best

Cherish™
Romance to melt the
heart every time

Desire™
Passionate and dramati
love stories

Have Your Say

You've just finished your book. So what did you think?

We'd love to hear your thoughts on our 'Have your say' online panel
www.millsandboon.co.uk/haveyours

- Easy to use
- Short questionnaire
- Chance to win Mills & Boon® goodies